T0156962

About the Book

Tarell's story is one that couldn't have stayed hidden. He was both humbled in the sight of God through his innocence and abused in the blindness of many in their own ignorance. This story will evoke emotions ranging from sadness to joy, while making you laugh in between. In a world where movies and literature reign supreme, *Blind Innocence* offers a unique story that has yet to be portrayed, offering a refreshingly, new journey through the life of a troubled adolescent. Tarell is mentally challenged and has been through a lot in his young life, suffering abuse from both his biological mother and his adoptive mother, women in general, and society. Just when it appears as though things are finally starting to look up for Tarell, who after meeting his biological family, all hell breaks loose. What started out as a dream quickly becomes reality, and soon, it all turns out to be a nightmare.

Then he meets Debbie, a young girl who, among all the other women he came across, has a heart filled with compassion and sorrow after hearing his story. Debbie talks her mother into taking in the homeless Tarell, but more drama erupts when Debbie's mother, a conniving, Christian woman, uses his mental disability against him in order to pacify her insecurities, causing him to endure even more mental and emotional damage. But as they say, "What doesn't break you will only make you strong."

Blind Innocence shares a poignant glimpse into one man's life as he faces seemingly insurmountable odds and slowly tries to create a meaningful life.

After everything Tarell has been through, will he be broken, or arise, victorious and strong?

Blind

Innocence

A. Adams Jones

Blind Innocence

iUniverse books may be ordered through booksellers or by contacting:

iUniverse
1663 Liberty Drive
Bloomington, IN 47403
www.iuniverse.com
1-800-Authors (1-800-288-4677)

ISBN: 978-1-4759-0154-2 (sc)
ISBN: 978-1-4759-0156-6 (e)
ISBN: 978-1-4759-0155-9 (hc)

Library of Congress Control Number: 2012905198

Print information available on the last page.

iUniverse rev. date: 10/17/2016

But their minds were blinded. For until this day the same veil remains unlifted in the reading of the Old Testament, because the veil is taken away in Christ. But even to this day, when Moses is read, a veil lies on their heart. Nevertheless when one turns to the Lord, the veil is taken away. Now the Lord is the Spirit; and where the Spirit of the Lord is, there is liberty.

2 Corinthians 3:14-17

Reviews

Jones' debut coming-of-age novel chronicles a neglected and abused young man's quest to not only survive, but also thrive. Jones wrote the novel as a source of inspiration, not as entertainment. This volume, which will be followed by a sequel, ends with the author's prayer, whose words reflect the philosophy of her novel: "Lord....Your words have always been said to me that you would work it out, and not to forget to practice patience and let your will play out." Moving, if not always graceful, inspirational fiction. – **Kirkus Review**

Spotlighting the plight of an educable mentally retarded child of a single, drug addicted teenage mother, the author has provided a window into the world of mental disabilities and the concomitant poverty and abuse such a child can face. The theme of human depravity and aggression against the weak is made quite viscerally manifest. The characterizations and plot are gripping and realistic. -**US Review of Books**

A. Adams Jones's heart-wrenching novel Blind Innocence offers insights into the often tragic trials of living with a mental disability. Blind Innocence is a harrowing and hopeful novel that raises awareness about living with disabilities through the dynamic characterizations of its leading cast. A story of the strength of faith, forgiveness, and love. It imparts a keen sense of melancholy and pain. Counteracted with the power of faith and love, such elements result in a fresh take on the genre. -**Foreword's Clarion Review**

This story is well thought out, compelling, and the characters are generally believable. Blind Innocence will elicit readers sympathy, and the message of God's saving grace will no doubt resonate with fans of the Christian genre. -**BlueInk Review**

Dedications

This book is dedicated to both my beloved cousin/ sister Myra Redden and my sister Lorraine Brown Alexander... R.I.P.; I love you!

Also, to all who are close to my heart and have passed on: My grandparents, Granville and Ruth Adams & Lonnie and Rose Mae Brown. Also, my aunts: Prim Rose and Della. My uncle/father, Harold Redden, my cousin David Redden, Uncle Wolf Brown, Uncle David Cobin, cousin Antonio Cobin, cousin Jerome Cobin, cousin Leward Cobin, and my beloved friend, Troy Washington. R.I.P. I love y'all!!

Acknowledgements

First and foremost, I would like to thank you, God, whom I love and adore so much for adopting me into your family and teaching me your ways, which have changed me. If it weren't for you, I wouldn't be where I am today, doing the things I do. Without you I am nothing and cannot do anything effectively. Above all, everything good that I do, I dedicate it to you... I love you!!

To my husband Michael, a.k.a. (Swell), thanks for being my husband. What would I do without you? I thank God for you, *"Smile."* I've never in my life felt that I "needed" any man. I always felt that they were in my life only because I "wanted" them there, so it was surprising to me when I realized that I needed you. For the first time in my life I saw that I didn't have to fight alone, and whatever little hidden fears that were there, even behind the fights, were gone, and I felt a human's security, something I've never felt. And it was God who sent you to be my human hero... I Love You!

To my parents, Alfred and Dorothy Adams, I want to thank you for giving me natural life. Without you, there would be no me. Thanks for your love and everything you've taught me. I love you both very much, always and forever.

To my aunt Annie, you have been like another

mother to me. I love you and thanks for everything. You are one that can relate to my character when a lot of people can't. Many don't understand a lot of the things I do, but you encourage me to keep doing them no matter what. Thank You!

Thank you Aunt Dell and the rest of my Kansas family for being so kind to me during my stay in Kansas. I'm forever grateful. God bless you Aunt Dell and the rest of the Cobin family!

I would like to thank everyone who helped me put the *Blind Innocence* soundtrack together: OB, Pat, Maurice, Chain, my son Stephen, and all the artists on the soundtrack. Much love to you all!!

Thanks to Shaborn and Miz for answering all my editing questions; and to Michael, Tammy, Janna and Sonje for proofreading and helping me with the editing of this book. Love you all!!!!

I would like to acknowledge my children: to my oldest child, John, I still think back on the day God blessed me with you; it was one of the happiest days of my life. I love you so much. You're always in my heart, thoughts and prayers.

To Anthony, God has shown us that you are highly favored and that He has big plans for your life. "Never forget that day." Love You!

Destiny, God has brought you a long way and look at you today, "*Smile.*" I have seen your faith take off in these past couple of years, and I know that lately, it's been rough, but keep the faith and watch and see what God does in your life. "It's coming!" Love you!

Hakeem, God has allowed you to see and witness

many things. It's all for a reason and it's all for a purpose, His purpose. In due time, everything will be made clearer to you. Hang in there and keep seeking after God. I have many thanks to you, but I'll just say, thanks for helping me rehearse that song, it meant a lot to me because you know how much I love to sing. "*Smile*" Love you!

Stephen, my youngest child, you remind me a lot of myself when I was growing up in many ways. Stay motivated in your sports and in your schooling. You're on the right path. Stay focused and all of your dreams will come true. You are one that always takes God serious and that's such a good thing. Love you!

Chris, I can't forget about you. I want to thank you for being such a wonderful Godson and for always being there for me. You are no different in my heart than any of my own children. I love you dearly!

I would like to acknowledge my siblings; it's even more of them than the amount of my children. Lorraine, R.I.P. Freddy, Michelle, Cynthia, Samantha, Alfred, a.k.a (Shaborn), author of *My Brother's Keeper, Port City, No Fair Exchange*, and *Till Death do us Part*, Mark, a.k.a (Miz) author of *Bishop, Bulldog Crew, Hater's Animosity* and *G-Banks*. Love y'all.

To my nieces, and nephews: too many to name, but I just want to say I love y'all.

To my sweet precious grandkids... nana loves you! Princess, the mother of my grandkids, thanks for taking such good care of them. Love you!

Alexis, I'm looking forward to the new edition. I

know you will do a great job as well. I also want to thank you for all that you do. You have been there for me in more ways than you know. Love You!

I would like to acknowledge the Jones family; my other side of the family... love y'all!!

To the Washingtons, Thanks for embracing me when I came to CT over 20 years ago and made me feel like family, even today I am treated as family... Love y'all.

I want to thank you, Richard Barrett, Kim Brice, Tamara Burroughs and my attorney, Rick Altschuler for being a part of my life for over 20 years; y'all are very close to my heart. Love y'all!

Lilly, Larrisha, Brady, and Lava, you were some of the first people that heard this story while I was writing, and the ones that inspired me to keep writing. I just want to thank y'all for showing love; it meant a lot to me. Love y'all!

Chapter One

It was a miracle that Tarell Johnson was even born on July 22, 1984 to 19-year-old Monique Johnson and 20-year-old Paul Wright. Monique was young, unstable, and on crack, which she had been smoking since she was 17.

At 5'6 and 135 pounds, light pecan complexion, almond-shaped eyes with thick dark eyebrows and long wavy jet-black hair, Monique was considered very pretty. In fact, a "bombshell" is what the guys in her high school called her. Monique was very popular throughout high school and was voted most popular among her peers. She was funny, down to earth, outspoken, crazy, and had a great sense of humor. Aside from being very pretty, she was also considered one of the best-dressed females in her school. She had a lot of friends and was liked by many. As popular as Monique was, one thing that made her stand out even more than her looks was the fact that she didn't look down on people, no matter who you were. She didn't care whether you were popular or not or wore the same nice clothes she wore. If you wanted to be her friend, she was willing to become one. However, if you rubbed her the wrong way or violated her in anyway, she would become your worst nightmare; she was tough and didn't back down from anyone.

Paul was also very popular. He was a handsome, all-star football player for the high school team. He was brown skinned, six feet tall, and 170 pounds with a nice broad build. Paul was born to be an athlete and had big dreams for his future. He would tell Monique how he was going to one day make it to the pros, marry her, and take care of her. He was laid back and was the total opposite from Monique. Monique loved to hang out and party, but Paul would rather watch a good movie at home or a theater.

He would, however, accompany Monique from time to time when she partied. Paul had a saying: "A person didn't have to go along to get along." He didn't agree with a lot of things Monique did, but he loved her, and for that reason, he could still get along with her. They were like night and day, but they loved each other.

Chapter Two

M onique's experience with crack didn't get out of control until after she had Tarell. Although she had experienced crack on numerous occasions, she also sold crack for one of the neighborhood drug dealers until she got strung out and no one would put any more drugs in her hands. But because she was so good at hustling, she had many different ways of getting money. Monique was an undercover smoker; that's what they called 'em, because for a while she was able to hide her addiction. She kept herself together and didn't let her appearance go. But being undercover only lasted for a moment until her cover was blown. No undercover likes to smoke alone; there will always be at least one person smoking with you, and that very person will be the one to blow your cover.

Even though Monique still looked good and kept things together for a while, she was still looked upon as an undercover. Monique's response was typical, "Undercover? I don't think so."

As time went on and crack got the best of her,

Monique's cover was not only blown, but what was underneath now came to the surface. Family members tried to help Monique, but as much as they tried, they got nowhere, so they eventually left her alone. She left her mother's house and ran the streets.

Paul and Monique's relationship ended before Tarell was born. Paul was no saint, but he managed to keep himself together even after Monique drew him into smoking crack. He continued to work his job down at the local paper factory that an agency had got for him. Paul even applied for college after graduating high school but didn't follow through. Although Monique's life had already taken a turn for the worst before she learned she was pregnant, an abortion was not an option; she refused to consider such a thing. When Paul suggested it, she flipped out on him. At the time of the argument between her and Paul, Monique had already left her mother's house and lived from crack house to crack house, hanging out in the streets all night, hustling and doing whatever she had to do to make a dollar.

"Nigga, I know you ain't even trynna tell me to get rid of my baby." Monique spat.

"That's exactly what I'm telling you," Paul said. "You're two and a half months pregnant; you don't need no baby. You don't even have a place to live, out here running the streets and getting high. What happened to you? You had so much going for yourself, Mo."

"And I still do," returned Monique.

"And don't stand here and lecture me, Paul. You

ain't no saint, and you damn sure ain't better than me with your little factory job."

"Mo, I'm not gonna stand here and argue with you. All I'm saying is that you really need to consider getting an abortion. Neither one of us is ready to take on a child," Paul pleaded. "I'll be pursuing my college career again in a couple of months and I've already submitted my applications for some out of state colleges, so I'll be gone for at least four years."

"Go ahead! Me and my baby will be just fine," Monique said as she walked away.

Paul did just that. Within three months, he left for college and wondered whether the baby she was carrying was really even his.

Chapter Three

Even though Monique was on drugs and pregnant, it didn't stop guys that knew her from trying to get with her. These were guys that tried to get with her or wished they could have her during the time she wasn't on crack but couldn't. They felt that now was their opportunity, and all Monique would do is play them for their money by using her street game. She had the gift of gab and could talk her way into or out of anything. Some people viewed her as a con artist. She was so smooth; people didn't even realize they were being conned, even after they were conned and told that she was a con artist, they still didn't believe it.

When it was time to give birth to her baby, she was on the block with some of the other hustlers, standing around talking and selling crack. Suddenly, she began to feel pains in her stomach. She flagged down a cab and headed to Jamaica Hospital. This wasn't the closest hospital, but she didn't care much for the neighborhood one. Since she was into the street life, Monique didn't keep a lot of her scheduled doctor appointments. She would always have something to do in the streets that she felt was much more important than sitting in some doctor's office for hours waiting to be seen. Little did she know, had she kept those appointments, they could have possibly prevented the complications that lay ahead. Monique arrived at the hospital, huffing and puffing as her contractions came every three to four minutes.

"Can somebody help me? I'm having a baby!" she yelled.

A nurse responded from behind her desk. "Someone will be with you in a moment, so please take a seat."

Another contraction came, and Monique yelled, "I'm in labor and you're telling me to take a seat? No, I'm not taking no seat. If you don't get a doctor out here—"

Monique suddenly stopped, calmed herself down, and said, "Look, this baby is ready to come."

She knew that if she kept yelling, there might be a chance that the nurse would delay her further.

The nurse got up and said, "Follow me," and led Monique to one of the examination rooms in the back.

"Do you think you can manage to get undressed and put this gown on?"

"Yes," Monique answered, doubled over and holding her stomach.

While handing Monique the gown, the nurse asked, "Is this your first baby?"

"Yes it is."

"Oh, I see. Well, someone will be in to get some

insurance information from you, and a doctor will be in shortly to examine you."

"Okay," Monique said as the nurse left the room.

Every time a contraction came on, Monique would let out a yell. "Ohhh my God, please somebody get this baby out of me!"

After ten minutes of being in the room, a woman came in and said, "Hi, my name is Linda and I'm here to collect some insurance information from you. I need you to tell me your full name."

Through hard breathing, Monique answered, "Monique Johnson is my name."

"How old are you?"

"Nineteen."

"What is your full address?"

"567 Beach 19th Street, Far Rockaway."

"Okay," Linda said as she wrote down each response in her notepad and asked, "What kind of insurance do you—"

"Ooooh, God, please help me!" Monique interrupted as another contraction came.

"Could you please do this later? And where's the doctor?" Monique asked, holding onto the railing for dear life.

In that moment two doctors walked into the room.

"We were just finishing up," Linda informed the doctors. "Monique, I just need to know the name of your insurance company to put in the computer. I can get whatever else I need a little later," she added.

"I have State Insurance," Monique said. "My insurance is through the state welfare."

"Okay. Thank you, Monique, I'm just gonna need the card if you have it. I can come back for it."

"Yeah, I have it in my pocketbook." Monique pulled out the card and handed it to Linda.

"Okay, thanks; I'll just run a copy and bring it back."

"Hi Monique, I'm Doctor Paterson and this is Doctor Egan. We just need to examine you to see how many centimeters you are."

After a brief examination, Dr. Paterson said that Monique was three centimeters. Then he added, "A nurse will be in the room shortly to connect you to a monitor so that we can keep track of your heart rate, and we also need to get an IV going. We'll come in from time to time to examine you and see how much you're dilating."

At that time, another contraction came and Monique yelled.

"Aaaahh!"

"You're having another contraction, just relax," the doctor said.

"Please," Monique said, "you have to get this baby out of me! Why is it taking so long?"

"Your contractions seem to be coming maybe four to five minutes apart, but your water hasn't broken yet. You only arrived thirty minutes ago, from my understanding," the doctor said.

"Yeah, but thirty minutes is a long time when the contractions keeps coming so fast," Monique said.

"You're three centimeters and you have to dilate ten centimeters before the baby can pass through the cervix."

"Oh my God! How long is that gonna take?" Monique cried.

"I don't have the answer to that," the doctor answered. "Hopefully not too long, because I know you're in pain."

"Well, could you at least give me something for the pain?" Monique asked as another contraction came.

As the doctor was walking out of the room, he turned and said, "Let's just wait and see what happens. If I give you pain medicine, it will numb you and you won't be able to push. Just take deep breaths and try to relax when you feel the contractions coming on."

Relax? Monique thought to herself. *I'm lying here in all this pain and he's telling me to relax?*

Although Monique was thinking those words, she knew better than to say them out loud because the doctor was the last person she wanted to make her enemy. Both her life and her baby's life were in the doctor's hands.

Just as the doctors left the room, the nurse came back to start the machines to monitor Monique's heart rate and contractions and start her IV. After an hour of contractions, the doctors examined Monique again and told her that she was still three centimeters.

"What?! After all this time and I'm still three centimeters?" she cried. "Oh God, and I have to get to ten before the baby can come," she sobbed.

Monique held onto the bed railing, breathed hard and cried out, "Oh my God! This is my word; I'm not having no more kids!"

Chapter Four

No one in Monique's family knew that she was in the hospital having a baby, although some of her immediate family knew she was pregnant. Her siblings saw her out on the streets from time to time, and her mother had heard about it. Monique didn't go around her family much.

Monique's siblings treated her like the black sheep of the family, mostly because she was the only one that was in the streets and on drugs. Even though Monique's siblings looked down on her, her mother still loved her and treated all of her children just the same.

After ten hours of labor, Monique had only reached four centimeters. With her contractions coming on faster and Monique dilating very slowly, the baby started losing oxygen, so the doctors decided that they needed to perform an emergency C-section.

Because the medical staff was not prepared for this, it took another two hours to set up an operating room for the surgery. Even still, it would be a while before they could give Monique anything for the pain. Without question, the baby's life was in danger.

While in the delivery room as they began to perform the surgery, they first gave Monique a needle in her spine, a procedure they called a spinal tap. The needle they injected was so painful that it took five doctors to hold Monique down as she cried loud enough for those outside of the operating room to hear. The thing was, this was a very sensitive procedure. The outcome could very well cause an individual to be paralyzed if not done carefully, which meant the patient needed to keep very still.

After nine more hours in labor, Monique finally had her baby boy. The nurse cleaned him and handed him to her, and Monique held him in her arms, overjoyed. She looked at him, smiled and said, "Hi Tarell" as if she had already picked the name out while waiting for him to be born. She was very tired after so many hours of labor, but the smile remained on her face as she gave him back to the nurse.

The nurse took Monique to the room where she would stay for the remainder of her time in the hospital.

After examining the baby and taking all the required tests on him, they found crack in his system, contracted through Monique's drug use. However, back in those days, they didn't make a big deal out of it. Mothers that were on drugs were able to take their babies home with them, as there were no government laws that prevented mothers on drugs from taking their baby from the hospital. It didn't matter whether the mother had a place for the baby to live or not. Giving the hospital an address was mainly for insurance purposes to ensure they were paid, and if for some reason they weren't, they would have a lead on how to find delinquent patients.

After three days, Monique was ready to leave the hospital, so she made a call to Buddy, a friend of hers who also sold drugs.

"Hi Buddy; it's me, Monique. I need you to come pick my baby and me up from Jamaica Hospital. I also need you to pick up an outfit for the baby."

"Alright," Buddy said.

Monique had been a good friend of his for many years; they grew up in the same neighborhood. Although Buddy would dip and dab with the drugs from time to time, he was more into his money.

"Oh yeah, I also need you to pick up a car seat for the baby because you know these people ain't letting me take this baby outta here without one," Monique added as she half laughed.

"Don't worry, I got you. I can't wait to see little Tarell, but you owe me, Monique."

"Yeah, I'll let you be his godfather." Monique chuckled.

Buddy arrived at the hospital with a few bags of baby clothes and the car seat already secured in the back seat of the car. Monique was standing in the lobby looking out the big glass window with Tarell in her arms as one of the floor nurses accompanied her.

Buddy got out the car to help Monique as he smiled at Tarell.

"Wassup little man? Say hi to your godfather," Buddy said as he strapped Tarell into the car seat. He helped Monique into the car and drove away.

Monique stayed in one of the crack houses that she frequented. It was located in one of the neighborhood project buildings. As she arrived with Tarell, her home girl Stephanie yelled from the first floor apartment window.

"Hey Mo! Let me see the baby!" She made her way to the front door.

"Ooooh look at him. He's so handsome. He looks just like you," Stephanie said while reaching for him.

"Yeah he does, don't he? He's my little man," Monique smiled and handed Tarell to Stephanie.

"So how you feeling Mo? You been at the hospital for like five days."

"Tired, girl," Monique answered as she walked into the apartment living room to sit down.

"That's probably the most you've rested or laid up in years," Stephanie said as she followed Monique into the living room and sat down beside her.

"Oh you got jokes huh? I guess having this baby took a lot outta my behind. Anybody in the back room?" Monique asked Stephanie.

"No!" Stephanie responded. "There ain't been many people in here today; I guess ain't nobody got no money, but you know that don't stop us," she added. "Since when did either of us let that stop us from getting our smoke on?" Stephanie laughed.

Monique laughed, took Tarell from Stephanie and said,"Yeah I know that's right. Can you picture us not being able to get high? Even with us being broke. But, you know a sister knows how to get paid." With Tarell in her arms she continued, "Let me go lay this baby down and take a quick nap."

"Okay Mo," Stephanie said.

Monique headed to the back bedroom of the apartment. It had a single bed and a small 13-inch outdated black and white TV sitting on a milk crate, and no other furniture. The fitted sheet on the bed looked as though it hadn't been washed in weeks, and the flat sheet that was a pair to the fitted one was hanging over the bedroom window, being used as a curtain. Monique undressed the baby and laid him down beside her, and they soon fell fast asleep.

When Monique woke up, the baby was still sleeping. She went into the living room where there were other people sitting and smoking crack. The living room didn't have much furniture either. It had a dirty sofa that looked as though it wasn't fit for a dog to sit on, let alone a human being. The sofa smelled horrible, and had stains in it that resembled dried urine. There was also an old coffee table in the middle of the floor and a small chair in a corner.

Sean, a regular at the house, looked up from his cloud of smoke when he saw Monique enter.

"Hey, what's up Mo?" he said with a smile.

Monique's eyes went wide when she saw the crack pipe passed around. She wasn't paying Sean, Tasha or Sherry, who owned the apartment, any attention when she responded, "Hi."

"Here, Mo," Stephanie said, passing Monique the pipe she held in her hand.

After taking it, Monique put it to her lips and inhaled deep and long. After exhaling, she said, "Man, it's been five long days."

After about an hour of smoking with the others, Monique took Stephanie to the side and asked her to keep an eye on Tarell.

"Stephanie, I have to go out and make some money."

Stephanie took Monique's arm and said, "No, you need to go down to that WIC office and see if you can get some free milk for that baby."

Monique pulled her arm free and said, "Yeah yeah, I'll do that one day next week. In the mean time, I'll use the little bit of food stamps they're giving me next week down at the welfare."

Stephanie walked away laughing and said, "Yeah, that's if you don't sell them first."

"Girl, please; even if I do, I take care of mines. I'll be back in a few," Monique said, heading out the door as Stephanie headed back into the living room to continue getting high.

An hour had passed and Monique had not returned. Tarell woke up crying, and Stephanie went to the back room to check on him.

"Ooooh, what's the matter baby, is it that you need your pamper changed, or are you hungry? You're gonna have to help me out here cause I don't have any kids, so I don't know about this stuff. I hope your mother has a bottle in this bag."

Stephanie looked in his bag and saw five bottles

with milk in them, but the only one that had a nipple on it was almost empty. "Okay, here we go; just let me replace this nipple and put it on one of these other bottles."

She gave it to Tarell, and while holding him in her arms, she said, "I'm gonna take you up front with me and when you're finished with your bottle, I'll come lay you back down."

When Stephanie got to the living room, she sat on the couch with Tarell in her arms sucking on his bottle.

"Oh come on Stephanie," Sean said, "Why you bring Mo baby in here?"

"Because I didn't wanna stay back there, man, this is where all the action is. I wanna smoke too."

"I have a son myself," Sean said, "Least you can have some respect for the baby. He don't need to be in here."

"Sean, do me a favor and shut the hell up and pass that pipe."

Sean laughed, and said, "Whatever," and passed Stephanie the pipe.

Chapter Five

Monique had Tarell outside with her even though he was only a few days old. Most times, she took him with her everywhere she went. When she was on the block she would have Tarell sitting right beside her in his carseat while she hustled.

As time passed, Monique became more addicted to crack and lost her looks. Her appearance was bad. Even the guys who used to try to get with her no longer gave her the time of day. Everyone except Monique saw how bad things had become.

Her family began to complain because she had Tarell out with her in the streets and living in crack houses. Nobody called child welfare even though they knew what was going on. However, after nine months of Monique's neglect, someone did call child-care services. When they finally caught up with Monique, they took Tarell from her. Monique flipped out yelling, cursing and crying. As they took Tarell away, she yelled, "Y'all don't have no right to take my baby! I had him; he came outta my womb!"

Stephanie and her friends tried to calm her down.

Since the police stood there with child welfare, Monique knew not to do anything stupid. When her friends were finally able to calm her down, she stood in front of the building and bawled as they took Tarell away.

The child welfare social worker took Tarell to the hospital and found out he was suffering from malnutrition and was severely underweight. They did not realize that Tarell's mouth was filled with sores until the doctor examined him. It was not known who called the child welfare, but the next day, Tarell's grandmother, Mary Johnson, found out through her other children that Tarell was in the state's custody.

Monique's mother was no joke. She was a strong woman and not one to be played with. Although she had four children by Monique's father, they never got married. Like Monique, Ms. Johnson had the same light pecan complexion, was 5'6 and petite, with long wavy black hair as Monique's, but the shape of her eyes was similar to that of Diana Ross. She was a beautiful black woman, indeed. Although she had not seen Monique's father since Monique's birth, he was ever-present in her life, as her kids all had his Asian genes. The pressure of a family was too much for him, so he took the easy way out and ran off with another woman. Although he left, Mary Johnson did what she had to do to provide for her children.

Ms. Johnson called the child's welfare service to see if her grandson was okay. They informed her that Tarell was in the hospital. When Ms. Johnson asked why, the social worker informed her that he was underweight, suffered from malnutrition, and had sores in his mouth, which caused a mouth infection. She also explained that a social worker was staying with him at St. John's Hospital.

Before hanging up the phone, the social worker asked Ms. Johnson if she would be willing to take Tarell into her home once he was released.

"Yes. That poor child, my God, I could only imagine what he's been through," said Ms. Johnson, wiping tears from her eyes as she hung up the phone.

Ms. Johnson got dressed and headed to the hospital. When she arrived, she went to the information desk and asked for her grandson's room number, then quickly headed for room 502.

"Hold up a minute, ma'am. I have to write you a pass. It's hospital policy."

"I'm sorry," Ms. Johnson said as she came back to the desk to get the pass.

"No problem; it will only be a second." While writing out the pass, the receptionist gave directions to the room.

"All you have to do is go straight ahead, and when you see the elevators, take it up to the fifth floor and follow the signs."

"Okay, thank you." Ms. Johnson turned and left.

Ms. Johnson had never seen Tarell before going into his room. She stopped at the nurse's station on the fifth floor and said, "Hi, my name is Ms. Johnson and I'm here to see my grandson Tarell Johnson."

"Oh, hi, Ms. Johnson. My name is Karen. Your grandson's nurses fell in love with him."

Ms. Johnson began to smile as Karen continued.

"His nurse, June, will be back shortly; she is on break. She'll be able to answer any questions regarding your grandson."

"Okay, thank you. It was good meeting you," said Ms. Johnson.

"Same here, Tarell's room is the first door on your left," Karen said as Ms. Johnson walked off towards Tarell's room.

Ms. Johnson entered Tarell's room and walked over to his bedside. She looked over him as he lay on the hospital bed on his back. He looked up at her with his eyes wide open, and she spoke softly. "Hi, sweetheart."

Tarell stared at her, as a child would do when seeing someone for the first time. He was Ms. Johnson's only grandchild.

"I know you don't know me, but I'm your grandmother," she continued.

Sorrow flooded her heart as she smiled, looking down at him. She hated seeing him in that condition. He had a feeding tube in both nostrils, an IV line in his arm and his hands were strapped down to each side of the bed posts so that he wouldn't pull the IV line out.

"I'm going to take you home with me, and I'm going to take good care of you. I know you've been through a lot being out in those streets, but grandma is gonna take care of you. You hear me sweetie? If it's the last thing I do," said Ms. Johnson as tears rolled down her face.

A nurse came into the room. "I'm June; you must be Ms. Johnson, Tarell's grandmother."

Wiping her tears from her face, Ms. Johnson answered, "Hi. Yes, that's me."

"How are you, grandma? Are you ok?" asked June.

"Yes, I'm okay," said Ms. Johnson.

"I know it's tough, but you hang in there," June said while checking Tarell's vitals.

"He's such a precious baby. We have been giving him fluids through the IV and feeding him through this feeding tube. He has sores in his mouth and the doctors are unsure of where they could have come from, but they are treating that as well. He's responding well to the medications and the doctors even suspect that he may be released as early as the end of next week, but we'll just take it one day at a time and see what happens."

"Okay, is there a certain time the doctor's come in the room each day?"

"Yes, they usually come in between 10 and 11 every morning. If you need anything, Ms. Johnson, you just ring," Karen said as she left the room.

Ms. Johnson then sat down next to Tarell and said a prayer while watching over him. Her spirit was full as she watched over her little angel, and started humming some old church hymns. The first was a song called "Blessed Assurance," and the other was "Pass Me Not, o Gentle Savior," both written by Frances Crosby, a blind woman from the early eighteen hundreds. As his grandmother sang, Tarell fell sound asleep.

Chapter Six

After that day in the hospital, Ms. Johnson made it her business to be there every hour of every day. It took a little over a month for Tarell to get better and get released. His stay at the hospital was longer than the doctors expected due to the sores that were still in his mouth. When Tarell was released, Ms. Johnson took him home. She fell in love with him even more as she watched him day by day, playing and depending on her to take care of him.

On Sunday morning while getting Tarell ready for church, Ms. Johnson, in her joy, spoke to Tarell saying, "You're such a precious child. So handsome. You look so much like your mama, with those pretty eyes and all that wavy hair. Now let's go to the Lord's house to get a good word."

After two months, Monique heard that Tarell was with her mother. She went over to her mother's house and knocked on the door forcefully.

"Who is it?"

"It's me, Mom. It's Monique."

"What do you want, Monique?"

"Open the door, Mom."

Ms. Johnson looked out the peephole and said, "I don't think you're supposed to be here with this baby here."

"Mama, open the door. I need to see my baby!" Monique started to bang on the door harder. Ms. Johnson opened the door.

Monique began yelling the minute the door opened.

"How are you gonna tell me I'm not supposed to be here and my baby's here? I came to get my baby!"

Monique walked from room to room looking for Tarell, and she found him in the back room of the house. As she picked him up, she kissed him and wrapped him in the blanket he was laying on.

Ms. Johnson yelled, "No! You leave him alone! Haven't you done enough to this little boy?"

Monique stomped out the room with Tarell in her arms. "He's my baby and he's going with me!"

Ms. Johnson grabbed Monique's arm, desperately trying to stop her from taking Tarell. Tarell started crying, scared from all of the screaming.

"Monique, I said put him down!"

"Move out of my way, Mama. Please don't make me do something I may regret!"

"Oh, now you're threatening me?"

"Get out of my way!" Monique yelled as she pushed her mother and tried to leave out of the house.

Ms. Johnson scuffled with Monique but didn't have the strength Monique had because of the age difference. Monique got outside and headed down the street with Tarell in her arms. Ms. Johnson was in tears. Some of her tears came from seeing how increasingly worse her daughter was becoming. She did not contact child welfare or the police to let them know what Monique had just done. Instead, she called her eldest daughter, Sharon.

Sharon, unlike Monique who was street smart, was book smart. Although you could tell Sharon and Monique was sisters, they did not look alike. Sharon had more of her mother's facial features opposed to her father's, but she did have her father's light complexion. She was 5'8, 140 pounds, had shoulder length wavy hair and was also very pretty.

When Sharon answered the phone, she sensed trouble in the tone of her mother's voice.

"What's the matter, Mom?"

Sharon became frantic after she heard her mother cry.

"Monique came and took Tarell. I was trying to stop her but I couldn't," Ms. Johnson cried.

"Did you call the cops?"

"No." Ms. Johnson continued to cry.

"Why not, Mom? You have to call them. You need to report it."

"No, Sharon; please let it go. I have to find Monique with that baby."

"I'll find her for you. It will be alright. I want you to relax, Mom; I will find her. Let me call Jackie so I can meet up with her. I'll call you back in a little while," said Sharon before hanging up the phone.

Sharon called her sister Jackie who is two years

younger than her but two years older than Monique. They also have an older brother named Patrick, but he was never around when they needed him. Sharon and Jackie met up and began looking for Monique. They knew most of the spots and areas she hung out in since their family lived in the neighborhood all of their lives. They approached Penny, one of Monique's crack-smoking friends.

"Hi, Penny," said Jackie. "Did you see Monique out here?"

Penny's eyes looked as if they were about to pop out of her head. You could tell that she had just finished smoking and was high. Penny looked around nervously and said, "No, I haven't seen her all day."

Jackie turned and walked away, knowing that Penny was lying. "Yeah right."

As she and Sharon searched the neighborhood, they ran into many of their old friends who had fallen victim to the streets and crack.

"Joe," Jackie called, "have you seen my sister Monique?" Joe smiled when he saw that it was Jackie and Sharon who had called him. He figured there was a good chance that he would be able to talk them out of a few dollars to buy crack.

"Oh, hi Jackie. Yeah, I just saw her about 20 minutes ago."

"Where did you see her?" Jackie asked.

"She was headed towards the projects."

"Did she have a baby with her?"

"Yeah, she was carrying a baby."

"Okay. Thanks, Joe."

Before Jackie and Sharon walked away, Joe asked, "You think one of you could loan me a few dollars until I get paid?"

Both sisters looked at each other, laughed and Sharon said, "Now you know you don't have no job, and no we aren't going to support your crack habit."

When Sharon and Jackie reached the projects, they spotted Monique standing in front of the building known as the "crack building" with Tarell in her arms.

"Give me the baby," Sharon said as she approached Monique. "You know better than to go over to Mom's house and take that baby from there. She should have called the cops on you. Look at you; you're off the hook for real."

With Tarell in her arms, Monique turned and headed for the door of the building.

"You ain't takin' my baby," said Monique.

"Yes we are! Monique, just give us the baby," interrupted Jackie as she went after Monique. "We're leaving here with the baby one way or another. See, Mom won't call the cops, but I will after I get finish whooping your ass."

"You wish you could, Jackie. Who do you think you are? All of a sudden you got heart?" asked Monique.

"Yeah, I do, and I'll show you just how much I have if you ever put your hands on my mother again."

Although Monique was on crack and her sisters were older, she was not scared of them. She had always been the tougher one, however, they were not scared of her either; they looked at Monique as a crazed crack head.

Sharon reached for Tarell and tried to snatch him from Monique. She was not trying to give Tarell up, so she held on to him tight as they struggled back and forth, arguing over Tarell as he cried.

Jackie jumped in. "Get off him!" she yelled as she worked Monique's hands from around Tarell.

In spite of Tarell being in Jackie's arms, Monique swung at her, hitting her in her face. A guy name Rasheen from the projects grabbed Tarell from Jackie as she charged towards Monique to fight back. Sharon tried to break the fight up. Those standing around the building cheered them on.

"Oh man, she snuffed her!" said a young guy in the crowd.

Monique had Jackie in a chokehold as she continued punching her in the head and face area.

"Get off of me!" Jackie yelled as she tried to break loose.

"Monique, let her go!" yelled Sharon as she tried to pry Monique's arms from around Jackie's neck.

Jackie broke loose and went crazy on Monique, swinging like a mad woman, landing hits in Monique's face then grabbing her long ponytail, refusing to let it go.

"Oh, they going at it!" laughed another guy in the crowd.

Sharon tried to get the two sisters apart, yelling, "Somebody help me! I don't believe this; everybody standing around watching instead of trying to break them up! They are sisters for crying out loud!"

Rasheen started yelling, "Call the cops somebody!"

Another guy who lived in the projects broke them up and pulled Monique back. Sharon and Jackie took advantage of the situation, got Tarell from Rasheen and took off with him.

Jackie was far from a fighter and as petite as she was, she didn't let that stop her—not this day, anyway. She was 5'2, 115 pounds, pecan complexion and looked exactly like her mother.

Chapter Seven

Sharon and Jackie brought Tarell back to their mother's house. However, no more than a week went by before Monique was back at Ms. Johnson's door, high on crack and causing a big disturbance before she took Tarell. Again, Ms. Johnson could not find it in her heart to call the police or child welfare. She knew Monique would more than likely be arrested for kidnapping.

Ms. Johnson loved her daughter and hoped that one day she would change her life. She didn't want to be a part of sending her daughter to prison, and felt it was the right decision she was making. However, Ms. Johnson loved her grandson, too.

So again, Sharon and Jackie went out to find Monique and after hours of searching for her, they found her and brought Tarell back to Ms. Johnson.

Monique would not stop. Again, she came by Ms. Johnson's house, causing disruptions and taking Tarell. As Tarell reached the one and a half year-old mark, Monique went over to her mother's house, more out of control than ever before. Ms. Johnson refused to let her in. Monique tried everything to get into her mother's house until one day she climbed through an unlocked window and took Tarell. Ms. Johnson, again, was on the phone crying to her oldest daughter, Sharon.

"I can't take it no more. She's never going to stop coming after Tarell as long as he's here."

Sharon was hurting inside because she did not like to hear her mother in pain and said, "Mom, calm down; we're gonna find him like we did the other times."

Sharon called Jackie and they went out looking for Monique and Tarell. This time they found Monique, but she didn't have Tarell with her. After an intense argument, she refused to tell them where Tarell was.

"Monique, where's the baby?" asked Sharon.

"Get out my face!" said Monique.

"Monique, where's the baby?" Sharon exploded.

"Sharon, I don't have time for this, and I'm not gonna tell you again to get outta my face!!" she demanded.

"If you don't care about your own life then so be it, but what has that baby done to you for you to be doing this to him? If you wanna smoke your life away then do it; my only concern right now is my nephew!" yelled Sharon.

"I am so sick and tired of y'all worring about my baby. Y'all need to get a life and leave me the hell alone!" Monique screamed as she pointed her finger in Sharon's face.

"Don't nobody care about you screaming. You ain't scaring nobody!" said Jackie.

"Come on, let's go!" Sharon said, speaking to Jackie.

After they searched for Tarell for hours, they went back to their mother's house only to report to her that they found Monique, but she did not have Tarell with her and refused to tell where he was. Ms. Johnson was trying to be strong while listening to the bad news, but it was obvious that she was worried about her grandson.

They waited hours for Monique to bring Tarell back. The phone finally rang. Ms. Johnson picked it up and said, "Hello."

A deep voice responded.

"Hi, my name is Mr. White. I am calling from the child welfare office. I am calling to inform you that we have your grandson here with us. I am the supervisor; one of the social workers here that worked on your case recognized little Tarell when he was brought in to us. He was found on an abandoned house porch. Someone spotted him sitting there and called the police."

Tears ran down Ms. Johnson's face, both from joy and worrying. "Oh my God!" she said. "Is he okay?"

"Yeah, he appears to be. Ms. Johnson, how did he get from your house to being on an abandoned porch?" Mr. White asked.

Even though she hated to say how, she responded, "He was with his mother."

"His mother? Why was he with his mother?" wondered Mr. White.

Through tears, she continued, "I can't do this anymore."

"Do what anymore?" Mr. White asked. "What are you talking about, and how did he get with his mother?"

Still in tears, Ms. Johnson said, "I can't keep him anymore. The best thing for that child is to put him up for adoption. Monique is not going to stop using drugs; she is not even trying to stop. Monique came over to my house to get him and I let her. I didn't know I wasn't supposed to."

"Okay, Ms. Johnson. Someone will be in touch with you. It will more than likely be the same worker that was already on the case."

Of course Monique was questioned about the incident, but had come up with some lame story about Tarell being with someone else at the time. Some unknown friend, whose nickname she only knew, and who was never found.

After hanging up the phone, Ms. Johnson turned to Sharon and Jackie and told them that they found Tarell on an abandoned house porch.

"What!" Sharon exploded.

"I told the supervisor who was just on the phone that the best thing for Tarell is to put him up for adoption," Ms. Johnson said with tears still running down her face.

"Why would you tell them that, Mom?" asked Sharon.

"It's the best thing for him. Monique is never going to stop coming after him as long as he stays in the family, and I'm scared something worse is gonna eventually happen to him."

"I don't know, Mom," Sharon said, and looked at Jackie for support.

"It's for his protection. The state will find a good family to place him with," Ms. Johnson said as she wiped tears from her eyes.

Monique had lost her parental rights after Tarell was taken from her. Aside from the state welfare being cautious in giving her back her baby, she made no attempts towards getting him back. She never showed up at any of the court appointments, and they weren't able to locate Paul.

Chapter Eight

A fter the paperwork, interviews, and being on the waiting list, a single mother named Ms. Thomas adopted Tarell. Ms. Thomas had three other children in her house. She had two boys whose names were Robert and Steven, ages seven and eight, and a little five year old girl named Lisa who she had recently adopted. Judging from first appearances, you would think that being a part of Ms. Thomas' family was the perfect thing for Tarell. She was a social worker, and the other children in her house had on their Sunday's best.

Ms. Thomas had another biological child, a girl, who died four years prior; she was the twin to seven year old Robert, and her name was Robin. Her death was ruled a homicide and Ms. Thomas' husband was serving a life sentence for it.

Mr. Thomas was a very abusive man when it came to his wife and his children. Although he never physically beat his kids, he would often get drunk and beat his wife.

It was May 23, 1982 when Mr. Thomas came in

drunk. All three children were in the living room watching TV when he started with what he called "playing with them." He stumbled his way over to where they were sitting and watching TV on the floor, and began talking to them with his words slurring.

"How's my babies?" he mumbled drunkenly. "Come to daddy," he continued while reaching for Robin as the other two ran to hide.

The children loved their father but were afraid of him in his drunken state. He picked up Robin who began to kick and scream as he swung her around in the air.

"Weeee, weeee," he slurred as he went around and around, stumbling.

Since he was so drunk, his head started to spin while he swung Robin around in a circle. He slipped and fell, and Robin flew out of his arms and right into the marble table where she hit her head. She was pronounced dead at the hospital.

Although Ms. Thomas loved her children, she didn't stop what her husband was doing to them whenever he came home drunk. She loved her husband but was extremely scared of him. She knew if she said a word, he would jump all over her.

Mr. Thomas wasn't the only one abusing the children; Ms. Thomas was as well. She didn't drink alcohol or do things compared to her husband, but she would get her belt and beat them without mercy. The beatings were constant, and the children were very scared of her, however, they *did* love her.

Mr. Thomas' lawyer argued that Mr. Thomas

was intoxicated and did not kill his daughter intentionally. He professed that falling with her was an accident. Although he made a compelling argument, Mr. Thomas was found guilty and sentenced to life without parole. This was in part because the autopsy showed bruises on the child prior to what happened the evening of Robin's death. It was never known whether the bruises were from the father who would throw the children around when he would come home drunk or the mother who beat them unmercifully. Mr. Thomas was the one who would take the weight. It never came to light what part Ms. Thomas played in the abuse of those poor children. Mr. Thomas stayed so drunk most of the time that he didn't even know that she was beating the kids.

However, because of the children's love and fear of their mother, they never said a word to anyone concerning the beatings. The court decided after the autopsy that Mr. Thomas was responsible for the old bruises that were on Robin's body and didn't arrest Ms. Thomas for her part in not stopping her husband's out of control behavior. She was viewed as a victim as well.

At Robin's funeral, Ms. Thomas seemed to hold it together pretty well. She showed strength as she always did in the eyes of people, but that night while in her bedroom, she wept as she thought about her daughter.

"God, give me strength," she cried. "God I need you, my baby... my baby."

Ms. Thomas was a woman that attended church and was deeply religious. She had been going to the same church for years. This was the same church Robin's funeral service was held.

Chapter Nine

TARELL TO JERMAINE

After Tarell was adopted, the adoption agency allowed her to change his name, for his protection, to Jermaine. Therefore, from the age of two, he became Jermaine Thomas.

Ms. Thomas took care of Jermaine as far as feeding him and giving him a roof over his head, but by the time he turned four, he was being abused. At six, the doctor's realized that Jermaine had some mental problems. Ms. Thomas sensed it when he was around three. At the age of three, he couldn't talk well. At times, it appeared as if he was in another world, far away from this one. He was very thin since he left his grandmother's house. The time he spent in the state's custody on the adoption list proved to be detrimental to his health. He didn't like to eat; he would take a couple of spoons of his food and wouldn't want any more.

At the age of four, he witnessed the other children

being beaten, and now he was as well. His young mind could not comprehend what was happening or why. He was punished, at times, for mental issues that Ms. Thomas didn't understand. The adopted children were beaten worse than the others.

On Sundays, while at church, when the boys would act up, Ms. Thomas would whisper in their ears, "I'm gonna kick your ass when we get home."

She didn't hold back with cursing at the children, even while in the house of the Lord. She would never curse aloud or around other people; instead, she would just whisper in the children's ears. She also smoked cigarettes on the down low, but because she was a churchgoer, she would not do these things out in the open because she had her reputation to protect.

When Jermaine was five, Ms. Thomas had beaten him with a belt and the buckle hit him in the forehead; blood gushed out of the gaping wound on his head. Ms. Thomas tried to stop the bleeding by putting a rag over the cut, but his head wouldn't stop bleeding. As she tried to wipe the blood from Jermaine's head, he just cried and cried. She knew that she had to get him to a hospital because the cut was very deep. While she was driving him to the hospital she leaned over to Jermaine and said, "Don't you tell anybody what happened. You tell them you fell, you hear me?"

"Yes," Jermaine said, still crying.

When they arrived at the hospital, the doctor asked him after stitching his head up, "What happened to your head?"

Before Jermaine could answer, he looked over at Ms. Thomas who looked at him with a mean face, and answered, "I fell."

Even though the doctor responded by saying, "That was some fall," he suspected something different and called a social worker in to talk to Jermaine.

When the doctor left out, Ms. Thomas sensed that the doctor didn't believe Jermaine, so she spoke to Jermaine briefly before the social worker entered.

"Listen to me. Don't you say a word to nobody. You just keep saying you fell, no matter what they say. You understand me? You fell outside while playing."

After ten minutes of waiting, social workers came in and asked Ms. Thomas to leave the room. As she was leaving, she gave Jermaine another mean look.

"Hi, my name is Sara. And what is your name?"

Jermaine just looked at her and didn't say anything.

"Okay, you don't feel like talking."

She moved in closer, looked at the cut and said, "What happened to your head?"

"I fell," Jermaine said.

"Are you sure nobody did that to you?"

"I fell," he repeated.

After not being able to get another word out of Jermaine she left the room and told Ms. Thomas that she could go back in there. Ms. Thomas knew that Jermaine had obeyed her as they gave her the hospital discharge papers. Jermaine left the hospital with fifteen stitches in his head, covered by a big white bandage.

While driving home, Ms. Thomas grew very upset and said, "You could have gotten me in a lot of trouble!"

When Jermaine didn't respond, she looked in the rearview mirror at him and said, "Do you know I could have gotten into a lot of trouble behind you? You could have caused me to lose the other kids, do you know that?"

Sitting in the back seat scared, he didn't say one word all the way home.

After arriving home, he put on his night clothes to go to bed, and fell fast asleep. He often got thirsty in the middle of the night, so after tossing and turning, he woke up to get some water. Ms. Thomas heard the kitchen faucet water running.

"Who the hell is that in the kitchen this time of night?" She yelled.

"Me, Jermaine," he answered. "I'm getting some water."

"Turn that damn water off and get your ass back in the bed and don't let me hear that water running no more!" yelled Ms. Thomas.

He remembered the earlier beating, so he went to bed thirsty. After that night, instead of going to the kitchen for water in the middle of the night, he would go to the bathroom and flush the toilet and acted as if he had to use it, but he would drink water from it.

Living in the projects with the rooms right next to each other, you could hear everything; it was as if you were in the same room. There were three bedrooms, a living room, kitchen and a bathroom in the small apartment. All three boys shared a room. Lisa had her own room and Ms. Thomas had her room.

Ms. Thomas abused Jermaine physically and mentally and would not buy him any clothes. The little clothes he did get came from the Goodwill store. The only clothes that didn't come from the Goodwill were his church clothes. Sundays were the only time he was happy because he would get dressed up in his new church outfits. Then after church and every other day, he was considered a bum. As far as school went, Ms. Thomas didn't care about how he looked. Only church mattered because she had to keep up the family's reputation.

By the time Jermaine got to the third grade, the other children would tease him. They teased him not only because he was in special education classes, but also because of the clothes he wore to school. He only had a few friends, and they were the boys that were also in his special education class.

After being tired of getting picked on about his clothes, he complained to Ms. Thomas and asked her to buy him some new things, but her answer was flat out "no." He then decided that the church clothes were the best he had, so he started wearing them to school. The children really teased him then. They would ask him, "Are you on your way to church, or are you that stupid that you don't know the difference between church and school?"

It didn't matter to Jermaine what they said about

him; he continued to wear his church clothes to school. He felt that even though they teased him, he liked the way he looked in his church clothes. Eventually, they named him Church boy.

Chapter Ten

JERMAINE GROWS UP

Once Jermaine reached the tenth grade, he grew up to be an extremely handsome young man. He developed a nice build, and he had his father's broad shoulders. He was 5'10, 165 pounds, and a born athlete. He played basketball and football. Because he was so good, he made the high school team for both sports. The girls started to take notice and were really feeling him.

In Jermaine's sophomore year, most females didn't know him, but they saw how fine he was. They noticed it on and off the court. Most females in the school would be present at all the games. Soon, all the girls were trying to get with him. Although he never had a girlfriend, he tried to get with them as well. He would take their numbers and he would call them, but after the first conversation, they wouldn't call him back. When he tried to call them, they would come up with an excuse why he had to stop. He didn't have any problems getting a female's number; it was after the first conversation that they realized he was slow, and they wouldn't want to be bothered. He was in the tenth grade with an IQ of a fourth grader, so in reality, he had the mentality of a child.

One day while practicing after school, his math teacher Ms. Kelly approached him and told him she needed him to stay after school to make up some past due work.

"I will call your mother and tell her," said Ms. Kelly.

"Okay, I'll be there as soon as I finish here," said Jermaine.

Before they could get started with the work, she said, "I have a better idea; we can go to my house and do the work there. I'll drop you off home afterward."

"Okay, and I want to thank you for helping me because I really need it," said Jermaine.

Unbeknownst to Jermaine, Ms. Kelly had other plans, and they didn't have anything to do with schoolwork. When they arrived at her house and walked through the front door, she kissed him in his mouth. Jermaine was shocked and scared at the same time. He had never been kissed before; not even Ms. Thomas kissed him in the way that a mother would kiss her child.

After seeing his reaction, Ms. Kelly said, "Relax, it's going to be okay."

She took him by the hand and led him into her

bedroom. As she started to undress him, she took off her clothes as well. She led him to her bed and then laid down, and with his hands still in hers she led him down as well. While in bed, she laid him on his back and got on top of him as she performed sexual acts.

Although the female students weren't trying to give him the time of day after learning that he was slow, Ms. Kelly had her eyes on him for a while, even though he was only 15 and she was 28. Ms. Kelly wasn't a bad looking lady; any male high school student would want to be in her class, and many of them did try to get in. She was drop dead gorgeous, standing at 5 feet 4 inches, 125 pounds, with a light brown complexion and hazel eyes to compliment her short Halle Berry haircut.

Ms. Kelly was gorgeous, but she had low self-esteem, and was what some would call, "damaged goods," meaning she was beautiful on the outside but very much damaged on the inside. However, she never had a problem getting any man, but she always attracted the same kind of men: "Wannabes!" These were guys that *wanted* to be men, but they just didn't know how to, and because of this, they treated her badly.

Ms. Kelly had issues. Even though she was attractive, men in her age group whom she had been involved with, saw her as unattractive because of her ugly attitude. Ms. Kelly could never stay in a relationship, although she is a strong willed and independent woman.

It's one thing to be with a man that doesn't know

how to be a man, but it's another for him to be involved with a woman with these kinds of issues. These men didn't have the slightest idea how to correct their own issues, let alone deal with hers. So, they did what most "wannabe" men do: Leave! And it was because of the repeated rejections that Ms. Kelly had some major issues.

"Just relax and let me take care of you," said Ms. Kelly while having sex with Jermaine.

Jermaine was scared and didn't respond as she stroked him down.

"See, I told you it was going to be okay," she continued.

Jermaine had never felt anything so good before. He began to relax and respond back as Ms. Kelly rocked up and down. They both got so excited in the heat of passion that they both released at the same time. After three more times, she lay next to him and asked, "Did you like that?"

"Yes," said Jermaine as he stared at the ceiling, not knowing how to act.

"I take it you've never done that before, Jermaine."

"No, I didn't," he responded.

"Then let this be our little secret, okay?"

"I will."

After dropping him off at his house, she said, "I'll see you tomorrow."

That was the first of five more visits to Ms.Kelly's house in which they slept together. And every time they slept together she would give him a few dollars before dropping him off.

During the basketball season, the school played against a variety of local schools and Jermaine scored the top points for the team. He was even better at football. Ms. Thomas saw all the trophies, but she never found the time to go to any of his games. It did something to Jermaine to see all the parents there for their kids except his.

Chapter Eleven

It was also at the age of 15 when two women came to Jermaine's house and introduced themselves as Ms. Kent and Ms. Philip. They were representatives from the adoption agency.

They sat Jermaine down and told him that the agency felt it was time he knew that he was adopted. As they spoke to him, you could tell from the expression on his face that he was in shock from the news.

They handed him a folder with his family's information in it. He then realized why Ms. Thomas treated him as if he wasn't part of the family.

A sadness came upon him, and tears began to flow down his face. The two adoption workers watched him to see his reaction to the news and asked if he was okay, but he didn't respond.

As he continued to read, he learned that his real mother's name was Monique Johnson and his father's name was Paul Wright.

He learned that his mother was a crack addict and how she just left him on an abandoned porch at one year old, and how he was given to his grandmother Mary Johnson. The information went on to explain how his grandmother thought it was best that he be put up for adoption, although she loved him very much.

It mentioned how she would call the agency to ask about his well-being, and how she passed away from a heart attack a year after his adoption.

The report said that he had a little sister who was born three years after him who passed away at the age of one from neglect and malnutrition. It talked about how his biological mother was charged with criminal homicide and had spent time in prison for his little sister's death, and that she was sentence to 2 years in prison and 3 years probation.

Since Monique was a first time offender and a drug dependant person, the court was lenient and gave her the minimum sentence that the charge carried.

The adoption agency's policy was to keep track of his family members. The folder contained all of Monique's siblings and their last known addresses. It didn't have much information concerning his father's side of the family. It only had his father's name and age at the time Jermaine was born. It listed his last known address in the report.

After reading everything that was in the folder, he closed it and gave it back to Ms. Kent.

She shook her head and said, "No that's for you to keep."

"Are you alright, Jermaine?" Ms. Philip asked, seeing his eyes flooded with tears.

Jermaine looked at her and said, "Yes ma'am."

"Are you sure?"

He nodded his head and said, "Yes."

"I know this is a lot to take in but when an adopted child reaches a certain age, or when they are at an age where they can understand all this about their real family, we tell them."

As Jermaine stood up, Ms. Philip continued. "I have been working for this agency for a very long time and had personally gotten to know your biological grandmother before she died. She loved you so much and never stopped praying for you. Before she died, she shared with me why she felt it was best for you to be adopted. Your mother was sick, as the report states. She had a drug problem and kept coming around your grandmother's house taking you from there. Your grandmother felt you being adopted was for your protection, but she always wondered if she had made the right decision."

Ms. Johnson had peace after revealing the truth, but then later died with a worried spirit, not knowing if she had made the right choice for Jermaine.

When they were finished, the two agency workers left. Jermaine was so angry that he stormed out the living room and went into his bedroom. Within minutes, he came out the room and headed for the front door, passing Ms. Thomas in the kitchen.

Before he could get out the door, Ms. Thomas yelled, "Jermaine, get back in here. Jermaine, I said get back in this house."

Jermaine didn't pay her any attention as he headed for the project's staircase to get out of the building. He had the folder that the agency gave him in his hands. Using the money his math teacher, Ms. Kelly, had given him, he got on the train from Philadelphia to New York. When he got to New York he asked people for directions to get to the address of his family's house according to the information in the folder. He was instructed to take the A train going towards Far Rockaway, Queens and to get off at Mott Avenue, which was the last stop. He did as instructed. He came out the station, stood outside and opened the folder to look at the street address of the last known address of his family member's house. He walked and asked people to point him in the direction of Beach 19th Street. He looked at the street signs as he walked, but he was confused and lost.

He eventually found his way to the street of the house, but he couldn't find the actual house. There were people sitting on a porch laughing, clowning around and talking, but he was scared to ask them for help. After a while, he found himself walking in circles until it started to get dark. He walked back to the station disheartened because he could not find his family, so he got back on the train to Philadelphia.

When he got back home, as soon as he walked through the front door, Ms. Thomas yelled, "Where have you been?"

"I went to look for my real mother and family," Jermaine said.

Very hurt and very upset, she yelled, "Your mother? *I* am your mother! I raised you; we are your family! You're looking for a crack head that didn't even want you."

She got in his face and continued, "You got my last name... I raised you and you're talking about you're trynna find your real mother. Get out of my house! Get your stuff and get the hell out of my house! And don't come back! You hear me? Get the hell out of here!"

He went to his room and got all his clothes even though he didn't want to leave. Jermaine was scared and knew she meant what she said. He had no idea what his next move would be. He put what little clothes he had in a bag and left.

With no place to go, he wandered around for a while and then was directed to a men's shelter by a man on the street. Jermaine didn't like the way the shelter looked, nor did he like how it smelled. The shelter didn't look clean, it had a bunch of cots in one big room, and there were grown men lying on them. The smell was awful; it smelled like a bunch of grown men that hadn't bathed in weeks. The men kept coming around Jermaine, trying to talk to him. Although he spoke back, he really didn't want them around him due to their horrible smell. All of this was new to him, but he thought to himself that he had no other choice but to be there.

Before being officially signed in, someone from the shelter had to take some information from Jermaine. After interviewing him and learning that he was only fifteen, the administrator of the shelter contacted child welfare.

As Jermaine waited in the administrator's office,

a social worker from child welfare arrived shortly afterwards. The social worker contacted Ms. Thomas to make sure she was home and took Jermaine back to the house to find out what was going on.

They arrived at his house and sat down with Ms. Thomas who said, "He's out of control; he ran away because he don't want to listen to me. I can't deal with him. He's out of control."

Jermaine knew how mad she was and didn't put up a fight to stay at the house, even though Ms. Thomas was lying on him. She was upset and had manipulated the whole situation. The social worker assessed the scene and thought it best to remove Jermaine.

Jermaine was placed in a group home for troubled teenagers. He eventually experienced the same abuse in the boys' group home that he was subjected to at Ms. Thomas' house. He was mistreated by staff and had gotten into a few fights. Even though he didn't start them, he had no choice but to defend himself. This went on until he turned eighteen years old.

Chapter Twelve

JERMAINE 18

The group home released Jermaine when he turned eighteen. With no place to go, he called Ms. Thomas, hoping he would be able to go back home, but she refused, still holding a grudge. Jermaine didn't want to go back to the men's shelter; he remembered what it was like that day he tried to stay there when he was fifteen. He decided the only place for him to go was back on the A train in New York.

He figured he could sing to make money because he saw a man doing it that day when he was on the train. Jermaine knew that it was something about his voice that caught people's attention. Jermaine sang in the church choir ever since he was young. While at church when he was called on to sing, everyone would stand, clap, and carry on.

The first song he sung while on the A train was a gospel song called "Tomorrow" by gospel artists

Marvin and Carvin Winans. This was one of the songs he used to sing at church when he lived at Ms. Thomas' house. After he finished, all the passengers began to clap and put money in his folded down brown paper bag. He moved to another car when he saw the response, and he sang another church song. By the end of that day, he made close to four hundred dollars. He went to a clothing store and bought a couple of new outfits and a new pair of sneakers. With the money he had left, he bought something to eat.

That night, he slept in the train station on a bench. Well, he tried, but couldn't sleep. Out of fear, he had stayed up most of the night. Lying across the bench, he could hear the sounds of water dripping and it was dirty and dreary down in the station. By 4am, he was finally able to doze off. By 5am people were already in the station on their way to work. Jermaine woke up and hit the A train and again, he began to sing. Some were gospel songs, but he also sang some R&B songs he knew.

While singing a gospel song that morning called "I Need You Now" by gospel artist Smokie Norful, many tears were shed as the travelers listened; it didn't matter how high or low the note was, Jermaine could hit it.

He poured his heart into the song, and it was as if the people felt what was coming from Jermaine's soul. Not only did they feel what he was feeling and sensed what he might have been going through, but God was using Jermaine to minister to the people in song. It was as if Jermaine was speaking to God not only for himself, but also for the people in whatever they were going through.

When he finished singing, the people stood up and clapped as they gave him money. After moving to another car, Jermaine sang an R&B song that he grew up listening to when he lived with Ms. Thomas called, "How Can You Mend a Broken Heart" by Al Green. Although Ms. Thomas was a church-going woman, she didn't see anything wrong with listening to certain R&B songs like Al Green, who was one of her favorite. The church didn't know about Ms. Thomas listening to these kinds of songs. This was something Ms. Thomas did behind closed doors because it was against the teachings of the Pentecostal church she attended. The religious leaders of the church believed that listening to "any" kind of R&B music was of the Devil. However, Ms. Thomas didn't see it that way. As messed up as she was, she felt that anything positive—no matter who was singing it—was from God. She looked at Al Green's music as something positive; it brought back memories of the good times in her past, when she and Mr. Thomas were newlyweds.

As the days went by, Jermaine continued to sing on the trains and would buy himself a new outfit everyday and throw the one he had on in the train station trash can. Since he lived in the subway, he didn't want to carry the old clothes around with him. He continued to sleep on the trains and sometimes the station benches at night. He would wash up in the station bathroom in the middle of the night when there weren't many people in the station.

Singing on the trains gained him some popularity. People would give him their business cards and tell him to call. Most of the cards came from upcoming rap artists that were trying to make a name for themselves. After about two weeks, he was tired of being in the stations and on the trains, so he decided to call one of the artist's from a business card he had in his pocket.

He contacted an artist named B-Nice who agreed to meet with him. After talking to Jermaine, he realized that Jermaine was slow. He told Jermaine that he was a rapper and wanted him to sing back up on some of the rap songs he had written. Jermaine agreed to sing on the tracks and B-Nice took Jermaine to his studio to meet the crew. They laid down ten tracks together and Jermaine sung like a superstar. Since Jermaine spent most of his time in the studio, he didn't have time to sing on the trains to make money. It wasn't long before he was out of money and couldn't feed himself. He thought that B-Nice and his crew would give him something but they never did, and when he asked, they promised him something later, but later never came. After a while, Jermaine sensed that they had no intentions of giving him anything, not even food. He left, and from that day, he didn't go back to the studio. He was back singing on the trains.

Chapter Thirteen

One day, after he sung his third song, a lady approached him.

"Hi."

"Hi," Jermaine responded.

"You have a very nice voice," she said.

"Thank you," he returned.

"Oh, my name is Sheila."

"My name is Jermaine."

"So what are you doing out here?" Sheila asked. "I've seen you out here before."

"I don't have no place to go. My adoptive mother put me out because I went to look for my real mother," said Jermaine.

From the brief conversation, she could tell he had some mental problems. She looked at him with lust in her eyes.

"You're very handsome, Jermaine."

"Thank you." Jermaine smiled.

"If you want, Jermaine, you can stay with me," she offered.

Still smiling, and now with excitement in his face, he responded, "I can?"

"Yes, if you'd like. I think it's messed up that you're out here homeless, and since I live alone, I don't see it being a problem."

"Thank you," Jermaine said.

She led the way and Jermaine followed. As they walked together, she thought about all the things she could do with Jermaine. First, she hadn't been with a man in a long time. She was 38 years old and unattractive. She was five feet six and weighed about 195 pounds. She was light complected with freckles all over her face. The freckles made her look like she had chicken pox.

Jermaine had grown to six feet tall and 185 pounds of muscle. He had a caramel complexion, pretty lips and pretty teeth. His hair was short, wavy, and jet black. He had his biological mother's shaped eyes and thick eyebrows. Jermaine's good looks made it easy for Sheila to ignore the fact that he was mentally challenged. She had her own agenda. She had created her fantasies and desires, and Jermaine was the right man in her mind to fill them.

Jermaine complimented her on her house as they approached it.

"Thank you! And call me Sheila. It's okay for me to call you Jermaine, right?"

"Yes," Jermaine answered.

She led him into the house and as soon as they walked through the front door, Sheila began to undress him. He wasn't scared or nervous this time around because he had been with a woman before. He was just happy that Sheila was letting him stay there, so he would do whatever she wanted him to do. Sheila enjoyed herself since it was a long time since she had had sex, especially sex three times a day, but she was a woman who grew tired fast.

After a month, Shelia was through with him and told him he had to leave. Jermaine was shocked.

"Did I do something wrong?" he asked.

"No, you didn't do anything wrong; it's just time for you to leave. I'll be in touch from time to time if you're still in the station," said Shelia.

With no place to go, he went back to the A train. Sheila would go look for him whenever she wanted sex. While in the subway, and after two weeks had passed, another woman walked up to him after he had finished singing and said, "Hi, don't I know you from someplace? You look familiar, what is your name?"

"My name is Jermaine."

"You don't remember me?" asked the woman.

"No," Jermaine said.

"Let me stop," she continued, "you don't know me, but I would like to get to know you," she said.

Jermaine didn't respond.

"You're young and fine. Are you looking for a sugar momma?"

Jermaine was confused because he had never heard of a sugar momma.

"Huh? What's that?"

"You know, a sugar momma. Someone to take

care of you. What are you doing out here in the subway singing?"

"I'm trying to make some money because I'm homeless. I don't have no place to live; my adoptive mother said I can't come back to her house."

"Wow, that's mean. Why?" the woman asked.

"I went looking for my real mother and she got mad."

"Oh, that's crazy. So you're really homeless?"

"Yes," Jermaine responded.

"You don't look homeless."

"But I am," he said.

"Well my name is Karen and here is my number. Call me later, and maybe you can come by my house."

"Okay," Jermaine said.

"Don't forget, Jermaine." Karen gave a little smile then began to walk off.

He looked down at the number and said, "I won't forget."

Jermaine ended up losing her number, but that next day she was back in the train station looking for him. After she found him, she approached him.

"Hi Jermaine."

"Hi."

"What happened? I thought you were gonna call me?"

"I lost the number," Jermaine said.

"Is it that you just didn't want to call me?" Karen asked.

"No, I'm sorry; I was gonna call, but I lost it."

"Okay, I believe you. Let me give it to you again."

Karen wrote her number down again and gave it to him. Later that day, he called her. He could tell that she was happy to hear from him as she gave him her address and directions and told him to come over. He didn't have to leave the A train because it went right to her house. Karen had already sensed that Jermaine was slow, but she was only after one thing and that was his body.

She was 41 years old but looked as though she was 51; dark skinned with medium length dreads, five feet four, and 90 pounds with no shape at all. Jermaine arrived at her house.

"Hi, come right in. You hungry?"

"No, I already ate," he said as he glanced around the apartment, not wanting to make eye contact.

It wasn't long before she led him to her bedroom and started undressing him. Jermaine was getting the hang of sex and started to become very skilled, mostly because all the women he had been with were older and had showed him what they liked him to do to them. With him being young and an athlete, he had a lot of stamina and could go all day and night. Jermaine remained at Karen's house even after that day.

Karen was a Christian; well, that's what she claimed to be, so we'll just leave it at that. Jermaine would go to church with Karen, and she would tell him not to tell anyone about him and her. She would introduce him to the church members as her nephew. She would be in church shouting, dancing and carrying on, then they would leave church and go home and have sex the rest of the day.

Karen was also involved with an older married man that would come over to her house occasionally. When he would come over, Jermaine would have to stay in the other room. Sometimes he would even wake up from sleeping and hear them. He didn't know if Karen had told the man who he was or what, or maybe the man didn't even care who he was. Jermaine tried to follow Karen everywhere she went as if he was her child. She didn't like that, and would often make him stay in the house.

One day, Karen was leaving out to go to the store, when Jermaine tried to hurry and put his sneakers on so he could go with her. She stopped him at the door and said, "Boy, you're like a shadow. I can't even breathe in this house without you right there. Everywhere I go you want to go."

"I'm sorry, I just wanna go because I don't be having anything to do while you're gone but watch TV."

"Well... watch TV then. I'll be back."

"Alright," Jermaine said.

Since he was so needy, his stay with Karen didn't last long. She got tired of him after two and a half months. She came home one day and unexpectedly told him it was time to go.

Chapter Fourteen

Although three years had passed, instead of heading back to the A train to sing, Jermaine decided he would try to find his family again. He got off the A train at Mott Avenue and went to the street of the last known address, according to the paperwork in the folder. This time, he found the house. It was the same house that he passed three years ago where the people were sitting on the porch laughing and clowning around. There was nobody sitting on the porch this time, so he was able to see the number on the door. Jermaine didn't know it, but the people that sat on the porch that day were some of his family members, and he walked right past them. The house had been his family's home, but his aunt Sharon was the only person who lived there now. Jermaine held the folder in his hands; he had kept it safe with him from the time it was given to him by the agency. Jermaine rang the doorbell.

When his aunt answered and opened the door, he spoke confidently.

"Hi, my name is Jermaine. I'm looking for my mother; her name is Monique."

Sharon recognized the name Monique but was thrown off when he said his name was Jermaine. Sharon continued to look at him with a puzzled look on her face.

"Huh? You're looking for Monique?"

Seeing her confusion, he said, "My name used to be Tarell Johnson, but I was adopted when I was a baby."

"Oh my God!" she shouted. "Come in! Come in!"

"Oh my God, look at you," she said, now overwhelmed and overjoyed. She gave him a big hug. "Sit down! How did you know to come here?" Sharon asked.

Jermaine was all smiles. "The adoption agency gave me this folder when I was 15 years old." He handed her the folder.

Sharon took it and browsed through it.

"Hold on a minute, Tarell—I mean, Jermaine—I need to call your uncle. Give me a minute."

Sharon picked up the phone off the table and dialed her brother Patrick. After he answered, she said, "You're not gonna believe who's here! You better get over here. Come now!"

Sharon's 13 years old daughter Shaniya heard all the commotion and came into the living room where the two were. Sharon introduced Shaniya to Tarell.

"Shaniya this is your cousin Tarell, Monique's son. It's a long story, I'll explain it to you later."

Tarell and Shaniya greeted one another by saying hello.

Patrick arrived and knocked on Sharon's door.

"This must be your uncle now," she said as she went to answer the door.

Before Sharon could say anything, Patrick spoke saying, "What's going on, Sharon?"

Patrick came in, and with Jermaine standing there beside her, Sharon said, "You know who this is?"

"Well, he looks like us, but who is he?" Patrick answered.

"It's Tarell, Monique's son!"

Surprised and happy to see Jermaine, he went over and hugged him. "What's up man? It's good to see you! How are you?"

Jermaine fought back tears as he felt the love he was missing all of his life. "I'm fine, thank you. It's good to see you, too."

Jermaine started blushing. *So this is what love feels like,* he thought to himself.

"Do my mother live around here?"

"No, she lives in Laurelton. It's not too far from here; I'll take you there to see her," Sharon said as tears started to form in her eyes.

"I'll go with you," Patrick said. "You have a sister that's eleven years old; and hopefully sometime today, you'll meet my two kids, Bobby and Britney whose 15 and 14. Your mother lives with her boyfriend, which is your sister's father. But just to warn you ahead of time...your mother is crazy. Not crazy as in insane, but crazy as in wild."

Sharon laughed and said, "Don't pay him no mind. Your mother was always "streetie," but even at 37 years old and not into the streets anymore, the streets are still in her. She's the only one of us that was into the streets, and she still got a lot of game."

Patrick looked at Jermaine and laughed at what Sharon said, then added, "She's my sister and I love her, but we don't really mess with her. Besides, she hardly comes around the family."

Although Patrick was close with Sharon and Jackie, he was a private person who was into whatever it was he was into, and whatever he was into he kept it to himself, but he always kept in touch with his two sisters.

Patrick was a light skinned husky guy who stood at 5'11 and 230 pounds. He wore cornrows straight back coming halfway down his back and had very little facial hair.

Chapter Fifteen

JERMAINE TO TARELL

While driving to Monique's house, Sharon and Patrick questioned Jermaine about his upbringing. They wanted to know a little about who cared for him and where he lived. Jermaine filled them in on some things about where he grew up, who adopted him, what school he went to, and how many siblings he had. He didn't get to tell them a lot about his past life because the ride to Monique's house was only 20 minutes.

Once they arrived, Sharon knocked on her door.

"Who is it?" Monique asked.

"It's Sharon and Patrick," responded Sharon.

After Monique opened the door, she said, "Hi. So what brings you two over here?"

"We brought someone to see you."

Sharon moved out the way, and Jermaine stepped

from the right side of Sharon where he was hidden and said, "Hi."

Monique was confused as she looked at him, but said, "Hi" in return.

"You don't even know who he is, do you Monique?" Sharon asked.

Before Monique could say anything, Sharon continued, "That's your son, Tarell."

"Tarell? That's Tarell?" Monique asked, surprised. "Oh my God, my son!" Monique was at a loss for words. It had been so long since she had seen her baby, and she never thought she'd see him again.

As Jermaine gave his mother a hug, Sharon jokingly said, "Wow... you didn't even know who he was when you said hi to him."

Monique laughed and said, "It's been a long time. I was caught off guard. I kind of gave up years ago; I thought I would never see him again."

Sharon and Patrick stayed at Monique's house for about an hour then Sharon said, "We have to be getting back, so we're going to let the two of you get to know each other."

Jermaine got up and hugged Patrick and Sharon.

"Will I see you later?" he asked.

"Yeah, you will," Patrick responded.

Before leaving, Sharon wrote her phone number down on a piece of paper, gave it to Jermaine, and said, "I don't know what your mom is going to do, if she's going to keep you over here with her or if you even plan on staying around, but just call me and let me know what's what."

As she handed Jermaine the number, he put it in his pocket and said, "Okay."

Monique was so happy; she couldn't believe Jermaine was there after so many years apart. "Let's go in the kitchen so I can cook you something and we can talk," she said.

As they walked into the kitchen, Monique said, "Look at you! Wow! You're like my twin! You look just like me; you are so handsome!"

Jermaine smiled and said, "Thank you."

When they got in the kitchen, Monique continued, "What would you like to eat?"

"Anything," he answered.

"You like fried chicken?"

"Yes!"

"Well I guess that was a dumb question, who don't like fried chicken? Before I put this food on come go with me outside; there's a few people I want to introduce you to," said a happy Monique.

As she took him outside to introduce him around, she said, "You know you have a little sister."

"Yeah, Aunt Sharon told me."

"Oh okay. She'll be coming home from school soon, and she's gonna be happy to meet you."

Jermaine was overwhelmed by everything that was happening. He had always hoped for this day. "I can't wait to meet her."

Monique saw her friend Sabrina as she and Jermaine walked down the street.

"What's up girl?"

"Nothing much," Sabrina answered, "on my way to this bus stop to wait for Keith's bus."

Keith was Sabrina's six-year-old son. As the two were speaking, Sabrina wondered who it was that Monique had with her.

"Sabina, meet my son, Tarell,"

"Your son?"

"Yes, my son," Monique responded.

"Get out of here. Your son?"

Laughing, Monique said, "Yes my son. His name is Tarell. Don't he look like me?"

"Yes, he does; all these years I've known you I didn't know you had a son!"

"Yeah, but it's a long story, I'll talk to you later," said Monique.

"Me and your mother been friends for years," Sabrina said to Tarell. "Well anyway, it's good meeting you!" she continued.

"It's good to meet you too," Tarell said with a smile.

After introducing Jermaine to some more neighborhood friends, they went to the store for food and headed back to her house.

After all the years in the streets and using crack, Monique was still very attractive. After she came out of prison, she left the drugs alone and soon found out she was pregnant with her daughter, now eleven years old. A person that didn't know Monique from the past would never believe she was once on drugs. She still had her long jet-black wavy hair and hadn't put on much weight from her teenage years. Monique didn't look much older than a teenager. In Jermaine's eyes, she was the most beautiful woman he had ever laid eyes on.

After they got home, Jermaine sat at the kitchen table while Monique took the food out of the bags and washed her hands. She took out the pots and began to cook.

"So Tarell, tell me something about yourself 'cause we have a lot of catching up to do."

"My adoptive mother changed my name to Jermaine."

"I see... well even though Jermaine is a good name, I like Tarell better, especially since I was the one who gave it to you."

Jermaine smiled and said, "I won't use the name Jermaine no more. I like Tarell better too."

"Did you graduate from high school?" asked Monique, glancing over at Tarell.

"Yes, I have my diploma. I was in a boy's group home when I was fifteen and I went to school there and got it. When I was in tenth grade, I was on the basketball and football team."

"A group home! Why were you in a group home?" Monique asked, startled.

"I came to look for you and my adoptive mother was mad and said I couldn't come back to her house."

Upset at the news, Monique started to say something but then caught herself after getting the first word out. "That—You know what? Let me calm down. So how long were you in a boy's home or group home?"

"Three years. I came out when I turned eighteen."

Still upset within, Monique said, "Okay, let's

talk about something else. So how good are you in basketball and football?"

"I'm real good; I won a lot of trophies."

"Oh, so you're *that* good, huh?"

"Yeah, I'm *that* good. And I can sing good too," Tarell said proudly.

"Oh yeah?" asked Monique. "Okay, so let me hear you sing something."

"Let me think about what I'm gonna sing." After about a minute he said, "Okay, I'll sing Amazing Grace; I used to sing that when I was at church."

Tarell sung for Monique better than he had ever sang before.

When Monique heard Tarell sing, it did something within her, but she tried to be strong and not get emotional.

When he finished, Monique said, "Oh wow, you can really sing! That was good; it's a gift, and I have it as well, and so does your little sister. I used to sing a lot when I was coming up, mainly in the church choir. They would always call on me to sing, and my momma was so proud of me."

In that moment, Monique thought about her mother and the memories of her childhood days.

"I would look over at her while singing and she'd be smiling and sometimes even crying."

In that moment, a smile came across her face, but you could see the sadness in missing her mother, even through her smile.

Just when Monique said that, Tarell's little sister, Ebony, walked in the door. Ebony didn't look anything like Monique or Tarell. She was short for her age, dark skinned, and she had thinly shaped eye brows, full lips, but had her mother's long wavy hair, which she wore it long in one ponytail. She didn't see Tarell or Monique, but only heard her mother's voice in the kitchen. She followed her voice and went into the kitchen, catching Monique off guard. Ebony saw Tarell and said, "Hi, Mom."

"Oh hi! I want you to meet someone. This is Tarell, your brother."

Even though Monique knew his name was changed from Tarell to Jermaine, she refused to call him that.

Monique continued, "Tarell, this is your sister, Ebony."

"Hi, Ebony" said Tarell.

"Hi," she responded back, but she didn't really understand what her mother meant when she said "her brother." Her mother never told her anything about having a brother.

"My brother?" she said hesitantly.

"Yes, your brother."

Ebony looked at Tarell and asked again, "You're my brother?"

Tarell stood up, gave his sister a hug and said, "It's nice to meet you."

"It's nice to meet you, too," she responded.

"What grade are you in?" Tarell asked.

"Sixth," said Ebony.

Monique spoke. "Ebony, I know I've never told you about Tarell, but he was taken from me when he was a baby and put up for adoption because I was so young and couldn't take care of him back then."

"So I *really* have a big brother." She smiled a wide, genuine smile.

Ebony and Tarell seemed to be hitting it off well. While Monique was in the kitchen cooking the food, they were in the living room playing with her Nintendo 64. Monique would glance over at her children in the living room from time to time and just smile at how well they were getting along. When the food was ready, Monique yelled, "Okay y'all; the food is ready, so go wash your hands!"

After washing their hands and heading to the kitchen, they both took their seats. Along with the fried chicken, Monique made baked macaroni & cheese, collard greens, yellow rice and candied yams.

"Give me one minute," Monique said as she took a batch of chicken out of the pan. "I always cook the chicken last so it won't be cold before the other food is finished cooking."

"Mom must be really happy to see you, Tarell, because she don't be cooking like this on no week day."

Monique didn't say anything; she simply smiled.

Chapter Sixteen

While they were in the middle of eating, Monique's boyfriend Rodney came in and saw Tarell. Without giving Monique a chance to explain who Tarell was, he automatically assumed that she had a man in his house. He walked over to Monique and started beating on her. She was trying to explain to him that Tarell was her son, but he didn't give her a chance to say a word. When she did get a word or two out between hits, he didn't pay her any mind, he just kept swinging until Monique was on the floor.

Tarell saw what this man was doing to his mother, and without thinking, he picked up the hot chicken grease off the stove and threw it in Rodney's face to protect his mother. Tarell then started punching and beating him, showing no mercy. Once the grease hit Rodney, he started to scream and tried to fight back, but it was no use because Tarell was young and strong.

Rodney wasn't a small guy, but he was short for a man. He was only 5'6, but he weighed around 195 pounds. He was solid. Rodney was Jamaican and wore his hair in dreads. Although he was a solid guy, he was slow with his hands; well that day he was, but he definitely lost some wind when the grease hit his face.

Monique staggered up off the floor and tried to pull Tarell off him yelling, "Stop it! Get off of him, Tarell!"

Ebony ran out the kitchen crying because even though Tarell was her brother who she had just met, Rodney was her father. The neighbors heard all the commotion going on in Monique's house and called the police. Monique finally managed to break them up, and was now mad and screaming at Tarell after seeing Rodney's face all burned up. Since he knew that the police and ambulance were on the way, Tarell knew that he was in a world of trouble. While Monique was attending to Rodney on the floor, she held his hand and began professing her love to him. "I'm right here baby, I'm not going anywhere, I love you." She paused, "If you would only believe me when I tell you that, then none of this would have happened." Hearing the sirens outside that was coming from the ambulance, she continued, "the ambulance is on the way."

Tarell remembered that he had Sharon's number, so he went into the other room and called his Aunt Sharon. Sharon answered on the first ring. Once she heard the way Tarell sounded, and knowing her sister, she knew something was wrong and asked, "What happened?"

Tarell explained that Rodney was beating on Monique, so he threw hot grease in his face and had beaten him up. Sharon dropped the phone and rushed out of her house to try to get over to Monique's, knowing the police would be there soon.

No sooner than Tarell hung up the phone, the police and ambulance arrived.

Monique yelled at Tarell. "You didn't have to do that; I can handle myself. That's my man you did that to; you had no right getting in the middle!"

"But he was hitting you," said Tarell.

"Why did you come here? You shouldn't have come here! Please leave and don't come back, stay away from here!" said a furious Monique.

The police walked in. "What's happening here?"

Rodney pulled a towel from his face and said, "He threw hot grease in my face, and I want him arrested. He assaulted me."

The emergency workers from the ambulance wheeled in a stretcher and placed Rodney on it. As the police looked at the burns on his face they turned to Tarell and asked, "What happened?"

"We was at the kitchen table eating and he came in and started beating up my mother and I was trying to protect her so I threw the grease on him."

Monique came over with her face bruised and her right eye blackened and said, "He hit me because he didn't know who Tarell was. I guess he thought Tarell was somebody I had just brought into his house. I never told him I had a son. Tarell was adopted when he was a baby. He came to my house today for the first time."

The police officer wrote down every word and said, "I'm not going to arrest him because if I was in his shoes, I would have probably done the same thing if I saw someone beating on my mother."

"Well he needs help," Monique said. "He's not in his right state of mind. What you need to do is take him and get him evaluated because he's not all there."

After talking to Tarell, the police officer thought that maybe Monique was right about getting him evaluated, so the officer got on the radio and called another ambulance to take Tarell for an evaluation at Queens General Hospital.

After the ambulance came and left, Sharon ran through the front door, breathing hard. She looked around at the three police officers that were in Monique's house and said, "What's going on? Where's my nephew?" Before either of the cops could answer, Monique spoke saying, "He threw hot grease in Rodney's face. It's all burned up. Let me go, I have to get to the hospital to be with him," said Monique.

"Ebony!" she yelled.

"Ebony!" she yelled again, and then walked towards Ebony's room where she was sitting on her bed crying. "Come on, sweetie, we have to go."

Ebony got off the bed and was led out the room by Monique. Sharon was in the hallway near the room as the police were still in the living room.

"I don't believe you Monique!" yelled a furious Sharon. "All you're thinking about is getting to the hospital to be with that no good boyfriend who beats on you every other day. What about your son? That man means more to you then your own son who you abandoned all those years ago, and now you're doing it again."

"Where's my nephew?" Sharon asked again, very upset.

With the police officer hearing Sharon, he came over to her and asked her who she was. It was the same police officer that had spoken to Tarell and Monique.

"My name is Sharon and I'm Tarell's aunt."

"Your nephew is on his way to the hospital," said the police officer.

"Why is he hurt?"

"No, he's going there to be evaluated."

"My nephew is not crazy; his mother is the crazy one. What hospital is he going to?"

"He's on his way to Queens General."

Sharon left the house, got in her car and headed for Queens General Hospital. While driving, Sharon called Patrick to tell him what happened. Patrick hung up and told Sharon he'd meet her at the hospital.

Jackie was at Patrick's house, so the both of them arrived together. By the time they got to the hospital, they all were very upset with Monique. As they entered the psychiatric unit of the hospital, Sharon asked a nurse standing behind the desk about Tarell.

"He just arrived not too long ago and the doctor has not had a chance to see him yet, but you can speak with the doctor if you'd like to find out if you can go back there," said the nurse.

"No, it's not necessary for us to go back there. We came to pick him up," Sharon said.

The doctor came out to talk to the three. When he approached them, Sharon said, "Hi, my name is Sharon and Tarell is my nephew. This is his aunt Jackie and his uncle Patrick."

"Tarell? Who's Tarell? The doctor asked, not recognizing the name.

"Well Jermaine," spoke Sharon. "We're here to pick him up and we don't plan to leave without him. He's not under arrest and you can't hold him in here."

"He's only here for an evaluation. I'm the doctor that will be examining him; I will be going in soon to see him."

"This is his mother's doing, but she has no authority to do this. She lost custody of him when he was a baby. He was adopted by someone else," Sharon explained.

"I'm going in to talk to him just to make sure he's okay after everything that has happened," said the doctor.

When the doctor finished talking to Tarell, he released him to his family members. Sharon and Jackie hugged him after seeing him and they could tell he was shaken up behind everything that had happened.

"Hi Tarell, I'm your aunt Jackie." Jackie hugged him again because she was so happy to see him.

"Hi, Aunt Jackie," he whispered.

"So what name do you like to be called by? I hear

them calling you Tarell, but your name is Jermaine," inquired Jackie.

"I'd rather you call me Tarell, because that's the name my mother gave me."

Jackie and Sharon looked at each other, smiled and said, "Okay, Tarell."

Tarell was sad and still shaken up behind what happened. As he got in his aunt Sharon's car, he was deep in his thoughts. He had always hoped for this day, but had no idea it would turn out like this. Within, he kept hearing his mother's words, "Don't ever come around here again; you shouldn't have come here."

Chapter Seventeen

Tarell went to stay with Sharon, hoping that everything would smooth itself out and he would be able to return to Monique's house and be with his family. That didn't happen. He stayed at Sharon's house for 3 months when he encountered a problem. Sharon and her husband already had plans to move down to North Carolina prior to Tarell's coming there. They had already bought a house and were just waiting to close on the sale. Sharon wanted to take Tarell with them, and spoke to her husband about it, but her husband was against it. Sharon argued with her husband back and forth for weeks, but got nowhere.

Two weeks before Sharon was to leave, she spoke to Tarell and told him how they had plans before he came back into their lives to move to North Carolina. She told him how she wanted to take him with them but couldn't, leaving out the fact that her husband didn't want him to come. She just told him they couldn't take him and she left it at that. Sharon was heartbroken about her husband's decision not to take Tarell. She was a stay-at-home wife and mother, and her husband made all the money and took care of all the bills. Sharon asked other family members if they could take Tarell in, but as much as they claimed to love him, nobody would. Tarell felt like they didn't really love him and had something against him because of their hatred for Monique. He knew they didn't like her and because he was her son, he felt a part of them didn't like him, either.

While at Sharon's house, Tarell asked her about his father's whereabouts.

"I'm not sure where your father lives, but he has a cousin that lives here in the neighborhood somewhere. I'll see if I can find out something as to where she is. What is Paul's last name?"

"His last name is Wright, Aunt Sharon."

"Oh yeah, that's right, It's just that I haven't seen or heard anything concerning Paul in years. He and Monique never stayed in touch I don't think, but I do know he has a cousin that lives out here with the same last name."

Since Sharon was a native of the neighborhood, she asked around that day and located Paul's cousin Yolanda. After meeting up with Yolanda and getting Paul's phone number, she gave it to Tarell.

Tarell didn't call his father right away, although he wanted to meet Paul. From the time he found out that he was adopted, he was ambitious and more focused on meeting his real mother. But after what had happened at Monique's house, he didn't move as fast to take the steps to meet Paul.

Three days before he was to leave Sharon's house,

he called Paul who picked up the phone on the third ring and said, "Hello?"

"Hello, can I speak to Paul Wright?"

"This is Paul."

"Oh, my name is Tarell, I was adopted when I was two years old, and the adoption agency gave me some papers that said my father's name is Paul Wright. My mother is Monique Johnson."

Paul was silent as he listened to Tarell. After what seemed like an hour but was only a few seconds, Paul said, "You said your name is Tarell?"

"Yes."

"Where are you?"

"I'm in Queens at my Aunt Sharon's house."

"Okay, Tarell. Can you meet me anytime tomorrow?"

"Yeah I can."

"Do you know your way around the Bronx?"

"No not really."

"What about Manhattan?"

"I know how to take the A train."

"Okay, then take the A train around four p.m. and meet me on 125th Street in the train station. Don't *leave* at four. I'll *meet* you at four," Paul said, becoming a little excited.

"Okay, I will be there."

"Tarell, just meet me at the token booth."

"Oh, you mean where the people pay the money to get on the train?" he asked.

"Yeah, that's right."

"Okay," Tarell said, and hung up the phone, feeling good.

The next day, Tarell arrived at 125th street about an hour early because he didn't want to be late. As Paul walked up to the token booth, he approached him and said, "Tarell?"

"Yeah, I'm Tarell,"

"Hi," Paul said as he stuck his hand out to shake Tarell's hand.

"Hi, Paul," Tarell said as they shook hands and stared at each other for a moment.

"You look just like your mother, but I can see me in you as well. You definitely have my height. How tall are you, Tarell?"

"I'm six feet."

"Do you play sports?"

"Yeah, used to when I was in tenth grade. I played football and basketball. I was on both teams and won a lot of trophies."

"Oh yeah... you're definitely my boy."

Tarell smiled but didn't know what Paul meant by that, but Paul definitely remembered having doubts about him being his son.

Paul continued. "So you alright, man?"

"Yeah," Tarell said.

"Well, it sure is good to see you."

"It's good to see you too," Tarell responded.

"So you're staying with your aunt Sharon?"

"Yeah, for now. She's going down south, but I can't go with her. I saw my mother Monique."

The moment Tarell said that, Paul cut him off in mid sentence.

"Please don't mention her name around me."

Tarell got silent.

"Well I'm not going to be able to see you after today, but I did want to meet you. I have a wife that I've been married to for the past 12 years, and we have kids together. I don't want to bring any confusion in my marriage. I mean, you're a grown man; I can see if you were a child."

Paul didn't even realize that his son had some kind of disability; he only focused on himself and couldn't see past himself and the life he already had. They shook hands, hugged and departed.

Chapter Eighteen

After Tarell left Sharon's house with no place to go, he tried to call Paul, but Paul had changed his phone number. So again, with no place to go, he headed back to the A train, where he would live and sing and make a living for himself.

While standing on the platform waiting for the train one morning, a guy walked up to him and said, "Hi, young man, my name is Cashmere; what's yours?"

"Hi, my name is Tarell."

"I've seen you singing on the train, and you have a beautiful voice."

Tarell said, "Thanks," but looked at Cashmere and thought to himself that something wasn't quite right with him. Since Tarell was slow, he didn't realize that Cashmere was gay at first. As Tarell continued looking at him, he noticed that Cashmere was dressed very well. He had on an expensive tailored suit, a diamond watch on his wrist, and some diamond rings on his fingers. His nails were well manicured, and not to mention he was a nice looking guy. As he stood in Tarell's presence and introduced himself, Cashmere looked at Tarell as if he wanted him.

"What are you doing out here so early in the morning?"

"I don't have no place to stay, and this is the time I always start singing. I have to sing to feed myself," said Tarell.

"I'll tell you what; you can come and stay at my penthouse. I have enough room for you and you can stay as long as you'd like."

"Thank you, Mr.," Tarell said with a smile on his face.

"Oh, please don't call me Mr. that makes me feel so old. Just call me Cashmere."

"Okay," said Tarell.

"You said your name is Tarell, right?"

"Yeah my name is Tarell. Well, it *was* Jermaine but that was the name my adoptive mother gave me, but I like Tarell better."

"Okay, Tarell it is! Now let's get out of this dreary filthy subway."

Cashmere's Penthouse was in midtown Manhattan on 57th street overlooking Central Park. Tarell had never seen anything like it in his life. The elevators opened right into the penthouse. It had a sunken living room with wall-to-wall white carpet and mirrors from floor to ceiling.

Cashmere was into the music business and knew a lot of famous people, such as, singers, rap artists and producers. He wrote music and had a lot of money.

As Tarell walked into the penthouse, Cashmere said, "You have to take your shoes off before you walk on the carpet, dear, so I hope your feet don't stink."

Tarell took his sneakers off and walked through the penthouse admiring everything. The kitchen was all shiny with stainless steel pots and pans hanging neatly in order by size and shape. The oven and stove were made of glass and Tarell wondered how could glass cooked food without melting.

Cashmere said, "This way to your bedroom."

Tarell followed him, taking in everything as he walked to his room.

Cashmere continued. "This is where you will be sleeping. This is much better than that train station, huh, Tarell?"

Cashmere smiled, as he looked Tarell up and down, then said, "Whatever you need I will make sure you get."

Tarell didn't know what to say because nobody had ever treated him like this. Tarell just smiled and said, "Thank you for giving me a place to stay."

Time went by and Tarell noticed that there were always alot of men sleeping over in Cashmere's bedroom. Some of the men that slept over were singers and rap artists that he was familiar with by seeing them on TV. There was even a producer friend of Cashmere's that he had seen coming out of Cashmere's bedroom one morning, half dressed. Tarell knew something was going on, but his bedroom was better than sleeping on the trains or even at the men's shelters, so he kept to himself. At the shelter, he remembered how there were many homeless men, sleeping on filthy, nasty, cots in a crowded room, and how bad they smelled. In the subway, he remembered it being cold at times and dreary, but felt that at least in the subway he could find some place down there where he could have his own spot without bums surrounding him.

Being in the penthouse, he witnessed alot of gay activities going on, but he didn't get involved; however, he would always accompany Cashmere to all the gay bars every weekend. Cashmere would often tell Tarell that he was going to speak with some of the famous people he knew about getting Tarell a record deal, but although Cashmere promised this, he had no intension of making good on his promise.

Being friends with Cashmere meant all Tarell's needs were met. He had a roof over his head and a nice one at that. He had expensive clothes, plenty of food in the kitchen and a little money in his pocket and didn't have to sing, although he loved to. After being at Cashmere's Penthouse for four months, one night, Cashmere came in drunk and tried to seduce him. When Tarell rejected him he gave Tarell two choices: to get with it or to get out. Tarell didn't want to go back on the streets, and he didn't want to live on the trains, so he got with it. Even though it was only a one-time thing, after that night, Tarell left and didn't look back. He would rather live in the subways and be on the trains singing than to be a part of that life. Although, there were times while he slept in the subway, he thought about going back, but he just didn't have it in him to sleep with men.

Chapter Nineteen

August 5, 2003

Tarell sang his way into the hearts of the passengers on the A train. People started to notice and expected to see him every day as they rode to work. That morning after leaving Cashmere's house and while on the train thinking about his mother and everything that had happened, Tarell sung a song called "One Last Cry" by Bryan McKnight. As Tarell sung, tears streamed down his face. The passengers loved the song, and they tried to hold back their emotions as tears came down their faces as well. Tarell wiped his tears after he finished his song. He felt good about himself and decided he would go to Macy's Department Store on 34th Street to get something new to wear. While he looked for his outfit, he saw a girl glance over at him, giving a little friendly smile. He smiled back at her, feeling the warm friendliness in her smile. She moved closer, looking at the clothes that were near him and as she crossed his path, she said, "Hello."

Tarell looked at her, smiled and said, "Hello."

She continued to look at the clothes, and after a minute said, "Excuse me, but I was wondering if you mind telling me how this dress looks."

She held it up against her body. Tarell looked and said, "It looks nice. I like it a lot."

"Thank you," said the girl. "They say if a lady wants to know how something looks, the best opinion is a man's opinion." She put the outfit to the side, picked up another and continued, "Oh, my name is Debbie."

"Hi, Debbie. Debbie is a nice name."

"Thank you, and yours?"

"Tarell."

"Tarell is a nice name; I like that," she said.

"Thank you," said Tarell.

"Well, it was nice meeting you. Are you shopping for yourself?" she asked.

"Yes, I'm looking for a nice outfit."

"Oh. If you want, you can ask me my opinion on something." Before he could say anything, Debbie said, "Those pants in your hands are nice," then, pulling a shirt from the rack, she said, "I think I like this shirt right here with those pants in your hands."

She pulled another shirt from the clothing rack and said, "I like this, too." She held the pants and shirt up against him.

"Yeah, that one is nice. I'll get that one, thank you," said Tarell.

"You're welcome," she said as she gave a little smile.

Before Tarell could head to the register to pay for his clothes, she said, "Call me sometime," and reached her hand out to give him her number.

Tarell took the number, put it in his pocket and said, "I'll call you real soon."

"Don't just take my number saying you gonna call and you don't call."

"When do you want me to call?"

"Anytime. Call me tonight if you're not busy."

"Okay," Tarell said as he headed to the counter to pay for his outfit.

Debbie was a beautiful 18-year-old female. She appeared to be very classy because of how she walked and talked, and even the way she dressed with her white collared designer shirt and her fitted skirt that came right above her knees, accompanied by some matching high heeled shoes. She was 5'7, 130 pounds, light skinned and looked as though she could pass for Puerto Rican because of her complexion and dyed red hair.

That night, Tarell called Debbie from a pay phone. Debbie answered on the second ring as if she was waiting for him to call.

"Hello, can I speak to Debbie please?"

"This is she." Debbie smiled as she recognized Tarell's voice.

"Hi, this is Tarell."

"I know who this is. So you *did* call me, huh?"

"Yep," said Tarell.

Debbie paused, and then said, "...So, are you from New York?"

"No, I used to live in Philadelphia with my adoptive mother, but I left to look for my real mother. When I went back home, my adoptive mother said I couldn't stay there."

"Oh, you're adopted?"

"Yeah, but I needed to find my real mother."

"I hear that. So when you went looking for her... did you find her?"

"At first I didn't when I was fifteen, but I found her a few months ago."

"Oh, so what happened?"

"It didn't go too well, but I don't feel like talking about it."

This was the first time he didn't want to talk about his past.

"Okay, so do you live in New York or Philadelphia?"

"New York," he said, "but I don't have no place to live, so I sleep on the trains."

"On the trains?" Debbie asked, surprised. "Are you serious?"

She sensed that he was a little slow, but it didn't matter to her. "How are you eating?"

"I know how to sing, so I sing on the trains and make money to eat and buy me an outfit every day."

"I can't believe your adoptive mother put you out because you went to look for your real mother. That's crazy; what's the matter with her?"

With so much compassion in her heart and feeling sorry for Tarell, Debbie said, "I live in Connecticut and I know you don't know me, but if you want, I'll ask my mother if you can stay with us. Just call me tomorrow and I'll tell you what she said."

"Alright," he answered.

Debbie and Tarell hung up. That day after hearing what Tarell shared with her, it weighed heavy on Debbie's heart as she couldn't get it out of her thoughts.

Chapter Twenty

The next day, Tarell called Debbie. He could tell that she was happy to hear from him.

"Hi, Tarell," Debbie said with excitement in her voice. "I spoke with my mom and told her your situation, and she said you can come stay with us!"

"I can?" Tarell responded in disbelief.

"Yes, you can," she said.

"Let me tell you how to get out here," she continued. "Do you have a pen so you can take down the directions?"

"No, hold on a minute," said Tarell.

Tarell put the phone down to ask someone for a pen. After a minute or so, he came back to the phone.

"Debbie, are you there?"

"Yes I'm here. Okay, what train are you by?" she asked.

"I'm at the A train on 59th Street," he said.

"Okay, ask around and find out how you can get to 34th street. You have to go to Grand Central Station on 34th Street," Debbie instructed. "You know what, Tarell... It will be better if you could just get in a cab because 34ᵗʰ Street is not far from where you are."

"Okay, there's alot of cabs up stairs outside." said Tarell.

"Do you have enough money to get in a cab?"

Tarell dug in his pocket to count his money, and then said, "I have eighty dollars."

"Okay, get in a cab and tell the cab driver to take you to Grand Central Station, and then get on the Metro North train going towards New Haven, CT." She continued, "When you get on the train stay on it till you get to Milford; that's the stop right before the last stop."

"Okay." Tarell wrote down Milford on his piece of paper.

"You won't get lost. Just stay on that same train, Tarell, 'til you hear the conductor say Milford. I will be standing there waiting for you."

"Okay," he said as he listened to Debbie's instructions.

"When you get your ticket, call me so I can know what time your train will be arriving."

"Okay, I will."

Once Tarell purchased his ticket, he called Debbie and told her the time his train would arrive. After he hung up, he got on the train and tried to relax. As soon as he closed his eyes, the conductor announced, "Milford," then continued, "Don't forget to take all your belongings and have a nice day."

As he got off the train, he saw Debbie waiting for

him with a big smile on her face. She walked up to him with her mother and introduced them.

"Hi Tarell. This is my mother, Tina. Mom, this is Tarell."

"Hi, Ms. Tina."

"Hi Tarell, please don't call me Ms. Tina. Just call me Tina."

"Okay," Tarell said.

Debbie didn't look anything like her mother; Debbie's looks must have come from her father. Tina was 44, about five feet five, close to four hundred pounds with an uneven dark complexion. Underneath both eyes were very dark circles, even darker than her two-toned face. She was sloppily dressed and her shoes leaned to the side. This was a result of her being knock-kneed. She was so knocked-kneed that when she walked she rocked from side to side and looked like she was going to fall at any moment. The only thing Tina had going for herself was her short wavy hair, which didn't do much good.

After getting in Tina's car, they headed towards the house, which was in Derby. When they arrived at the house, they all went inside. Tina had three other children. Debbie was the oldest of the four; she had two younger brothers. Carl was fifteen, Michael was sixteen and her little sister Shakira, who her family called Kira, was eight. Debbie introduced Tarell to the rest of the family. They each had their own bedroom and Tina had the big bedroom in the back.

"Debbie," Tina called, "I want you and Kira to

sleep together in your room and give Tarell Kira's room."

"Come on, Mom. No! I don't want Kira sleeping in my room."

"You heard what I said, Debbie. I don't mind Tarell being here because of his situation, but you invited him, so either you're gonna let Kira sleep in your room or you gonna sleep in her room and give Tarell your room. Take your pick."

Tina turned to leave the room and went into another room in the house. Debbie turned to Tarell and said, "I ain't paying her no mind; I'm eighteen with a job and I pay rent to her. It's not like I'm staying here for free, so she can't be acting like that. Where else did she think you were going to sleep?"

Tarell didn't say anything because he did not want to get in the middle. He was just glad to have a place to stay. And just as Debbie said, she didn't pay Tina any mind. Kira slept in her own room, and Debbie invited Tarell to sleep in hers, in the same bed. Although they shared the same bed, they slept on their own side of the bed, but that only lasted about a week.

After a week, they became intimate. Debbie seemed to be into Tarell, and Tarell liked her as well. She treated him nicely and they did things together. They went out to the movies and out to eat. They laughed and had fun being with each other. Debbie loved Tarell's voice and would often ask him to sing to her while they were in bed at night. Two of the songs Tarell would sing to Debbie, was a song by Babyface called "Every Time I Close

My Eyes" and the other song was "Love of My Life" by Brian McKnight. Those songs became two of Debbie's favorite songs. As time went on and without saying, Debbie's feelings grew deeper for Tarell and his grew deeper for her as well. Tarell had got a job working at night at a local supermarket as a stock person. Although he had never had a job before, it wasn't hard for him to learn it. All he had to do was lift heavy boxes and place them on the shelves. When he got paid, he started paying rent to Tina as well.

One night, Debbie was at the mall shopping with friends and Tarell was off, so he decided to watch a movie. While he was in the living room, Tina came in and sat next to him.

"What are you watching, Tarell?"

"I'm watching the movie 'Friday.' "

"Oh, do you mind if I watch it with you?"

"No, I don't mind."

They sat and watched the movie, and the next thing Tarell knew, Tina was trying to kiss him. Tarell didn't know what to do; he knew he didn't want her kissing him nor did he want to kiss her, but he knew he didn't want to get put out either. As Tina forced herself on him, Tarell pushed away because he really did not want to kiss her.

"Tarell don't act like you've never kissed before," said Tina. "You don't find me attractive? You can be honest with me. I know I'm a big woman and might not look attractive to a lot of men, but what do you think? How do you see me? Do you think I'm attractive?"

Not knowing what to say, Tarell said the only thing he thought she wanted to hear.

"Yes."

As she kissed him again, he couldn't fight her off without being so obvious, so he kissed her back. After kissing him and getting a response, she led him by the hand to her bedroom. Tarell was scared but also shocked and sad within. He was scared because he didn't know what to expect. He had never slept with a woman this big before and was shocked because he thought she was different from all the other older women that came on to him and gave him a place to live. He was sad as he thought about Debbie. He considered Debbie to be his girlfriend and he didn't want to hurt her, but he was more scared than anything that if he didn't do what Tina said, he was going to be back on the streets.

Once she got him into her bedroom, she started ripping his clothes off. She was turned on by his looks and body from day one. After his clothes were off, she looked him up and down and took her clothes off, then climbed on top of him, squashing him. She inserted him inside her. It didn't take long before he flipped her onto her back so he could get on top of her. He satisfied her until they both fell asleep. Tina stayed asleep, but it didn't take Tarell long before waking up, nightmares usually did it all the time. He woke up hoping that it was just a bad dream but then saw Tina lying next to him asleep and knew it really happened.

Tarell got out the bed and went into the bathroom and took a shower. He scrubbed himself in disbelief, not being able to accept what had just happened. As the water ran over him, he held his head down under it and he felt awful. All he could think about was Debbie. After he got out the shower, he went to his bedroom to go to bed.

Debbie came from the mall and went straight to her room where Tarell was in bed.

"Hey Tarell, you woke?" Tarell didn't answer. "Look what I brought you," she continued, but Tarell said nothing.

She took her clothes off, leaving the stuff she brought in the bags, showered and got in bed. Tarell pretended to be asleep. He was feeling guilty and did not want to face Debbie, not tonight, anyway. Debbie snuggled her body close against his, wrapped her arms around him, and went to sleep.

The next Saturday, Debbie was invited to her friend Ronda's birthday party and asked Tarell to accompany her. He was not used to going to parties and didn't care much about being around that type of crowd, so he stayed home. If she had invited him anyplace else, he surely would have went. The events that transpired that night made Tarell regret not going.

It was late, around 12:30am, and the kids in the house were asleep. Tarell was also asleep until Tina came in the room and woke him up.

"Tarell, Tarell...wake up," Tina said.

Tarell woke up and Tina made her way to his bed and with lust in her voice, she said,

"Could you do that to me again?" Now Tina was a woman that attended church regularly, and led the

Sunday morning praise and worship service. While they were having sex, she was calling out the name "Jesus" repeatedly.

After they were finished, she spoke to Tarell and said, "I'm in love with you." She paused, then continued, "Do you love me?"

He hesitated; he didn't know what to say, but since it was Tina's house, he knew he had better said yes. So, he said, "Yes."

Tina responded, "If you love me, I want us to get married so I can take care of you."

She pulled him closer to her and continued, "When Debbie comes in, I want you to tell her that you fell in love with me and want to marry me."

Tarell hated to have to do that, but he followed Tina's instructions and told Debbie just what she said.

Debbie was so upset she started crying and yelling, "Are you serious? You want my mother?" With tears running down her face, she continued, "I don't believe this; you want to be with my mother?"

Tarell saw how hurt Debbie was, but Debbie knew her mother was behind the whole thing. She went to her mother's room, and with the room door open Debbie entered, yelling.

"You slept with him, didn't you? Didn't you?"

"What are you talking about?"

"You know what I'm talking about! I don't even blame him; I blame you because I know you put him up to it."

"I didn't put him up to nothing; he told me the same thing he told you. He came to me telling me that he fell in love with me and asked me to marry him."

"I gotta get outta here," Debbie said as she stormed out of Tina's bedroom.

After that day, Debbie was more than ready to get out of Tina's house, so two months later Debbie and one of her girl friends got a place together. Debbie always had a soft spot in her heart for Tarell no matter what happened. Right before Debbie moved out, Tarell and Tina went down to the justice of the peace and got married. A month passed, and Tina became pregnant.

Chapter Twenty One

Pastor Davis' Sermon

People in Tina's church criticized her. Even the pastor wasn't in agreement with their marriage; he gave sermons on women in the Bible whose conduct was like hers. Tina knew he was referring to her, but she didn't care, or at least she acted as though she didn't. Pastor Davis spoke to his congregation saying, "Today's sermon is titled: Sex Scandals with Women in the Church."

Where there was more than a few "Amen's" from the congregation, Tina on the other hand, felt today would have certainly been the perfect day to stay home. However, she proceeded to listen to him preach.

"Turn to Genesis 38:11," said Pastor Davis.

"I'm not going to go into the whole story, but I just briefly want to read a little bit of the story of Tamar. Before I read, I want to tell y'all a little bit about Tamar. She was the daughter-in-law of Judah. She had married Judah's oldest son, but he ended up dying, and then she married another one of his sons, who was of age and also ended up dying." Pastor Davis paused.

"Man, it makes you wonder..." he began again. "Ok, church, does everybody have his or her Bible turned to Genesis 38:11? If So, Say 'Amen.'"

"Amen," said the congregation.

"Ok," said Pastor Davis.

"Let's get started reading," he continued.

"Then Judah told Tamar, his daughter-in-law, not to marry again at that time, but to return to her parent's home. She was to remain a widow until his youngest son, Shelah, was old enough to marry her, (but Judah didn't really intend to do this because he was afraid Shelah would also die, like his two brothers.) So Tamar went home to her parents. In the course of time, Judah's wife died. After the time of mourning was over, Judah and his friend Hirah, the Adullamite, went to Timnah to supervise the shearing of his sheep. Someone told Tamar that her father-in-law had left for the sheep shearing at Timnah. Tamar was aware that Shelah had grown up, but they had not called her to come and marry him. So she changed out of her widow's clothing and covered herself with a veil to disguise herself. Then she sat beside the road at the entrance to the village of Enaim, which is on the way to Timnah."

Pastor Davis stopped reading and said, "It's obvious to see, church, that Tamar was up to something."

"How many of y'all know that it's nothing worse than having a scorned woman on your hands; I'm talking to the men," he laughed.

"Verse 15... Judah noticed her as he went by and thought she was a prostitute, since her face was veiled. So he stopped and propositioned her to sleep with him, not realizing that she was his own daughter-in-law."

Pastor Davis put his Bible down and spoke saying, "I'm going to stop right there."

"Y'all can imagine the way Tamar must have been dressed. Now this was a widow woman, who dressed in widow clothing, the Bible says. So picturing what I'm assuming widow clothing to be back in those times, Tamar wore dresses down past her knees, flat loft shoes, head covered and not showing her hair. Now she's dressed in a short mini skirt up to her thighs, and a tight fitted, low cut shirt, panty hose and high-heeled shoes, showing her nice figure which was once hidden by her loose clothing. Tamar deceived her father-in-law, the Bible says... She was rejected and she felt betrayed and she was hurt by what had taken place in her past," he continued.

"She disguised herself just as women do today after being mistreated in their past. A part of them wants to move on, but then there's that part of them that feels as though they can't. How many know we can't follow after what we feel?" asked the Pastor.

"Amen, Pastor!" yelled a woman sitting in the back.

"So now the woman becomes one way, and then

another way," continued Pastor Davis as his voice went up a notch.

"That's why you can't underestimate a scorned woman. You never know what she's thinking or which way she's going to go. Not even Adam knew what he was dealing with when it came down to Eve; she was one way, then another. It was she, who deceived him. But what could she have been possibly hurt behind when she had it all. Being in God, she had everything and she didn't even know it. Blind, she became in the spirit, as her eyes were opened in the natural, seeing and doing things within the world, just like women today. But being in God, you don't allow things to hurt you; where they change you in a bad way," said Pastor Davis.

"But being a man, we know how weak we can get when it comes down to a woman. And with some men, the women don't have to be a beautiful woman within, or have a pretty face. She can have an ugly face, ugly attitude, with a banging body... come on church now, y'all know I'm talking right... can I get an Amen?"

"Amen, Pastor," said some of the church members.

"Lust doesn't exist only in a woman's pretty face. Let an ugly lady walk by with a nice body and see how many heads turn. Don't shout me down, men; y'all know I'm talking right. Amen, but back to my message. Tamar acted one way but then wanted people to see her in another way, like how you got some women in here coming to church acting like they're one way and then once they step foot out these doors, they are another way: very seductive and scandalous. Like Tamar, they slip out of their church clothes, and put on another kind of clothes. They try to put on holiness while at church, but then act like a prostitute when they leave the church! Amen? Y'all not hearing me church; can I get an Amen?"

"Got all kinds of sex scandals going on, in and out the church. Coming in my office trying to give me all kinds of gifts, making food for me, talking about how it was specially made just for me; you won't get me caught up in your sex scandals," said Pastor Davis.

"Yeah, Tamar had her reasons, but when you can't get past your past, in the things that happened in your past, being a churchgoer, you should know to go to God. God is calling the church to repentance!" he shouted.

As Pastor Davis continued with his sermon, the church members, along with the music coming from the organ, cheered him on. Tina sat there, but was tempted to get up and walk out of the church. However, she remained seated only because she didn't want the congregation to assume Pastor Davis was talking directly to her. Tina didn't view herself as scandalous and really didn't care to hear what Pastor Davis was talking about.

Who does he think he is? He got some nerves to be passing judgment on me or any other woman for that matter, Tina thought to herself.

Although Tina was angry inside, she played it off as she sat there with a straight face.

Chapter Twenty Two

D ebbie didn't hate Tarell, but she despised her mother. After a few months, Debbie would go around her mother's house every now and then to pick up her younger siblings or sometimes to just see them.

Eventually, she let go of some of the grudge against her mother, but their relationship was never the same. Debbie had a close-knit relationship with her mother before all of this, but now, she kept her distance. She did let her know in so many words, "I forgive you because you're my mother, but I will never forget."

Even though Debbie told her mother that she forgave her, that didn't stop her from sleeping with Tarell whenever she got the chance. Things like this happen all the time when a person can't move forward. You're not supposed to forget, meaning you don't sleep "on" the person. That's it, plain and simple. True forgiveness is paired with forgetting, not in a way where we try to convince ourselves that it never happened, but in a way where we don't feed into things. True forgiveness doesn't let what you're feeling inside get the best of you.

A part of Debbie wanted to sleep with Tarell because she had feelings for him, but it was also her way of getting back at Tina. Debbie didn't forget nor did she really forgive her mother, and the remainder of the grudge against Tina became present. The grudge in Debbie's heart grew, and when opportunity knocked, she indulged in it. But then there was a part of Debbie that felt that what she was doing with Tarell wasn't wrong because Tarell was her man to begin with. Tarell was happy during every moment that he got to be with Debbie, and he didn't feel guilty at all. Whenever they would have sex, Tarell always used a condom because he didn't want Debbie to get pregnant.

Being married to Tina was becoming hell for Tarell, but he stayed under her like a child stayed under his mother. He would want to go to church with her on Sundays, but since the church got on her so bad, she refused to take him. Whenever they would go around her family for events like barbecues or family holiday dinners, she would instruct him not to speak to anyone. She was afraid that he would embarrass her by what might come out his mouth because he was slow. Tarell didn't like it and was tired of being around her family and not being able to say anything, not even "Hi."

One day at a Thanksgiving family gathering, he decided to speak to Tina's mother.

"How you doing, Ms. Williams?"

"I'm fine; how you doing, sweetie?"

"I'm doing fine." That was all that was spoken between the two because Ms. Williams was busy entertaining the guests.

When Tarell and Tina got home that night, Tina went off on him.

"Didn't I tell you not to say anything to my family? You'll know the next time I take you somewhere."

"I'm sorry; I only wanted to say hi to your mother."

"I told you not to say anything, plain and simple!" Tina yelled.

"Why can't I ever get to say anything? I hate not being able to say nothing."

"Well next time, you just stay home."

"I'm sorry, Tina. I won't do it again. I promise." Tarell paused, and then said, "You mad at me? You're not gonna put me out are you?"

"Just don't do it again," Tina said, and walked away knowing that she had him right where she wanted him.

"I won't," Tarell said, following her out of the bedroom.

Tina was upset with him for hours. Tarell went into the backyard and picked a red rose and put it on her pillow, hoping it would cheer her up. Every time she would get upset, he would do this because he wanted to stay in her good graces.

Girls would check Tarell out whenever he and Tina would go out places. She would get mad, but what she didn't realize is that they thought she was his mother, not his wife.

Tarell had gotten laid off from his job. Even

though Tina was six months pregnant, upon hearing this, she put him out and said that she needed her space. He begged her to let him stay, but she simply said that she needed to be by herself for a while. She put him out after she spent all his money from his unemployment check, so he went to a shelter even though he didn't like being there and sleeping on a hard cot, but he had no choice. He called Tina the next day and told her he was at the shelter. After a week, she went to the shelter and picked him up so that he could go get his check and give her the money. After a month, she took him back in. By then, he didn't want to go back, but she was the closest thing to a mother, the thing he craved more than anything.

Although women slept with him up until they got tired of him, every woman he had ever been with always treated him like her child. Tarell was miserable with Tina, but he got used to being with her... and being mistreated.

One Sunday while Tina was at church, Tarell decided to take a walk outside. He had alot of things on his mind, mainly his biological mother. He couldn't get her out of his head. Almost two years passed, and he could still hear his mother's words ringing in his head. While walking, he went to a park and sat on a bench. As he sat in deep thought, a girl who was also sitting on the bench approached him.

"Excuse me, do you know what time it is?" asked the girl.

Tarell only heard part of what she said.

"Are you talking to me?" he responded.

"Yes, I just wanted to know if you know what time it is," the girl said.

"No, I don't have a watch."

"Oh, okay."

After a few more minutes passed, the girl spoke again. "You look like you came to this park for the same reason I came here."

Tarell just looked at her and said, "I'm just thinking about a lot of things; I have a lot on my mind."

"That makes two of us," said the girl. "I come here a lot just to think or just to get away from my dad because we don't get along. He's so strict. I'm sixteen going on seventeen and he doesn't let me do anything," she continued.

"And I just be thinking a lot about my mother," said Tarell.

"Something happened to your mother?"

Before Tarell could answer, she said, "Oh, my name is Tiffany, by the way."

"My name is Tarell."

They continued to talk. He began telling her some things about his mother and his life, and she continued to share more about hers.

Tiffany was very attractive. She stood five feet four, 120 pounds. She had a light complexion with long brown hair and deep dimples on each side of her cheeks. When she smiled, the dimples made her look even more beautiful.

Although Tiffany was beautiful, trying to get with her was the last thing on Tarell's mind. Tarell never had a real interest in any of the females that had come across his path, except Debbie. Women came on to him; he didn't come on to them. It brought comfort to him sitting on that bench just being able to have someone to talk to. After Tarell and Tiffany talked for a while, it started to get dark. They decided to walk and continued talking. Tarell ended up walking her all the way home. The thing with Tarell was that he would tell anybody who was willing to listen about his past and what was on his mind.

Once they got to Tiffany's house, she invited him in. One thing led to another, and they ended up in bed. Since Tarell had been with so many older women, he became good at "making love," but he also became a sex addict. Her parents weren't home and wouldn't be back until later that night, so Tarell stayed there with Tiffany until nine o'clock that night, and then went home.

As soon as Tarell got home, Tina started yelling.

"Where have you been?"

"I was just outside walking around."

"Don't give me that. Where were you?"

"I was just walking, and then I went to a park."

"Jermaine, it's nine thirty at night; don't tell me you were in the park. Please don't insult my intelligence!"

"Please don't call me that," said Tarell.

"If you don't tell me where you were, I'm gonna put you out!" Tina yelled. She only called him Jermaine when she was upset with him.

"I was at the park and I met a girl and walked her home."

"What girl?" Tina raised her voice up another notch.

"A girl I met at the park. I only walked her home."

"Do you think I'm stupid? Do I look like I'm stupid, Jermaine? Did you sleep with her?"

"No, I only walked her home." Scared, he continued, "I promise I'm telling you the truth."

"Okay, you telling me the truth? Well we'll just see about that. You gonna show me where the hoe lives. You walked her home, right... and found your way back home from her house, right? Well, you gonna show me where she lives, so let's go." Tina grabbed Tarell's arm then headed out the front door.

As they pulled up to Tiffany's house, Tina almost jumped out her car before it stopped. When she knocked on Tiffany's door, a male voice answered.

Tina looked at Tarell and said, "What is her name?"

"Please, let's just go home."

"I said, what's her name, Jermaine? Don't make me have to ask you again."

"Tiffany," Tarell said while looking at his shoes, refusing to look up. Tina looked at the man standing in the doorway and said, "Excuse me sir, is Tiffany there?"

Looking at Tina, the man said, "Why do you want Tiffany?"

"I need to talk to her. Is she your wife or your daughter?"

"She's my daughter. Now, what's going on? Why are you asking for my daughter?"

"I think your daughter slept with my husband but he's not saying so."

Tiffany's father yelled for her to come to the door. Before Tiffany arrived at the door, Tina asked her father how old the girl was.

"Tiffany is sixteen years old," he answered, and started to get angry as he looked at Tarell.

His answer surprised Tina and she asked, "Are you serious? Please don't tell me you slept with a sixteen-year-old girl, Jermaine. You're nineteen years old, soon to be twenty."

Tiffany came to the door, saw Tina, looked at Tarell and began to get worried.

"My name is Tina and this is my husband. He tells me he was with you today. Is that true?"

"Yeah," Tiffany said in a soft voice.

"Did you have sex with my husband?"

Tiffany started to cry and said, "Yes."

Tina continued and said, "Do you know my husband?"

Still crying, Tiffany said, "No."

"So why would you have sex with somebody you don't know? Somebody you only met today?"

Still crying, Tiffany said, "Because he's good looking."

"You slept with him because he looks good? That's crazy."

Tina looked at the father who didn't say a word while Tina grilled Tiffany with questions.

"I'm sorry for barging in on you like this," she

said. "And I'm sorry to hear about all this with your daughter."

Tina walked off with Tarell behind her, not knowing what she had just done. *Or did she?*

Three days later, Tarell was arrested for statutory rape. Tiffany's father was so upset that he forced Tiffany to say Tarell forced himself on her. Although it wasn't the truth, either way, Tarell would still have to pay the price. Sleeping with an underage person, whether by force or with the other person's consent, it's still considered rape.

When Tarell went to court the judge saw that he had no prior arrests and had some mental problems, and released him on a promise to appear. Tarell left court and went back to Tina's house.

Chapter Twenty-Three

A month later, Tina was ready to have their baby and Tarell went with her to the hospital even though she was not in labor. Once they arrived, Tina was escorted to the back. She had a private doctor from the clinic who worked at the hospital named Dr. Rivers. Tarell knew Dr. Rivers from his visits with Tina to her appointments. He wasn't allowed to go in the back with Tina; he was told by one of the nurses that he had to stay in the waiting room. After about 30 minutes, Dr. Rivers came from the back. Tarell saw him, then started walking towards him.

"Is my wife OK? Did she have the baby yet?"

Dr. Rivers recognized Tarell from the clinic appointments and said, "Mr. Thomas, your wife hasn't given birth yet. She is being prepped for surgery."

"She has to have surgery?" Tarell asked with a worried look on his face.

"Yes, she's not having a natural delivery. She didn't tell you she was having surgery?" asked Dr. Rivers.

"No, why is she having surgery instead of having it the regular way?"

"Son, your wife has a high level of HIV. It's almost in the AIDS stage and if we take the baby out through her vagina, the baby may be exposed to it. So we're going to take the baby out through her stomach. This is called a C-section."

Tarell was shocked and scared from the news Dr. Rivers gave him about Tina. He also learned that she had the disease for almost two years. That meant she married him and had sex with him even that first time, knowing she had HIV and she never mentioned it.

After three hours of being in surgery, she delivered a baby boy. Tarell went in to see her and held his son. He named him Tarell. He was so happy in seeing his son but couldn't stop thinking about what Dr. Rivers said. After they took Tina to her room and the baby to the maternity ward, Tarell went to be with his wife. While sitting with her, she looked over at him, smiled and said, "Your son looks just like you."

He smiled back as a proud father. Tarell didn't know if now was the right time to tell Tina what Dr. Rivers had said or what. He was happy about having a son; however, he couldn't stop thinking about what the Doctor had told him.

"Tina, Doctor Rivers said that you have HIV and that it's almost in the AIDS stage."

Tina started to cry. "Yes, I'm HIV positive."

Tarell felt sorry for her as he hugged her. Still crying, she hugged him back and said, "I'm sorry I didn't tell you. I love you, Tarell. I'm so sorry. Please don't be mad at me. Don't leave me. Me and the baby need you and you need us."

As he comforted her, Tarell hugged her tight and told her that he would never leave her.

Two months later, Tarell went to prison for statutory rape. In court the day of sentencing, the judge asked if anyone had anything to say before he passed sentence. Tina stood up and the judge said, "State your name for the record ma'am."

"My name is Tina Thomas."

"What is your relationship to the Defendant?"

"I'm his wife."

"Okay, you may speak."

"Your Honor, my husband wasn't in his right mind when he had sex with that girl. He act sometimes, well, a lot of times, on impulse and doesn't think, but he can't help it. Right before this happened I was in the process of taking him to get help because he needs it. I'm his wife; I know what I'm talking about, Your Honor. He needs to be on medication, and I think that as long as he's on medication he'll be fine. Please your honor, be lenient on him and allow him to be evaluated so he can get the help he needs."

"Thank you, Ms. Thomas; you may take your seat."

Tarell's attorney, Ms. Crane, got up to speak when Tina sat down.

"Your Honor, my client admits to sleeping with Ms. Brown. However, it hasn't been proven that my client slept with her by forcing himself on her. But he did plead guilty and is willing to accept the offer on the table. This was his decision, Your Honor; I just want to add that my client didn't know that what he did in sleeping with Ms. Brown was wrong. Thank you, Your Honor."

"Well, I do believe after hearing what you said, Ms. Thomas and also Attorney Crane, that an evaluation needs to take place as part of his sentence. Statutory rape carries a maximum sentence of 25 years in prison, but I'm going to order that he, Jermaine Thomas, serves one year in prison, five year's probation, and evaluation. If the doctor or doctors order him to be placed on medication, then as part of his probation he must abide by it." The judge looked at Tarell and continued. "When he goes into the prison to start his sentence, which will be today, while he's there they will evaluate him. If the doctor recommends medication, he will start taking it in there. When he's released, as a condition of his probation, the probation department and his doctors will supervise the medication. They will get together on that if it is the case after evaluation."

Tarell stood up, was handcuffed, taken to the back, and headed to prison.

Once he arrived, the prison conducted a mental and physical evaluation. It was determined that he needed to be placed on medication for depression and anxiety. While he was in prison, Tina never went to visit him. She wrote him from time to time and sent him money only twice for commissary.

After serving the one-year, Tarell was released and went home to Tina. His son was fourteen months old and Tarell was so happy to see him. He hadn't seen him since he was two months old. The best thing about coming home was he knew his son was there. Tina was all over Tarell as soon as he walked through the door. It had been a long while since she last had sex and Tarell had put on some prison weight which made him look even more sexy than before he went in. All Tarell wanted to do was be with his son, so he gave Tina what she wanted—to be left alone for a while.

It didn't take long after Tarell was out before Tina encouraged him to apply for Social Security Disability. The thing was, he had already been approved for SSI without knowing. His adoptive mother, Ms. Thomas, had gotten disability checks for him up until the age of 18, even though he hadn't lived under her roof since he was 15 years old.

At the age of six, Tarell was determined disabled by a Social Security Administration doctor with Educable Mentally Retardation, or EMR. This is a mild mental retardation. It meant that Tarell was capable of learning even in being mentally challenged. Normally, a person with this kind of disability doesn't need to take medication, unless there were some other things going on.

When Tarell turned 18, he was scheduled to attend an SSI hearing with Ms. Thomas to determine if he was still disabled, as required by law. Since he was not around to attend the hearing, he was no longer eligible for SSI and his checks were stopped. All this came out when he and Tina went down to the SSI building to put in an application. After Tina learned all this, beside the claim on the application for depression and anxiety, she reclaimed EMR.

Tarell was examined by the SSI doctor, and it was determined that he was EMR and suffered from depression and anxiety. He continued to take medication, and Tina received his checks every month. Tina also took him to the state welfare to apply for food stamps, and he was approved. Everything she wanted she bought with both her own money and his.

The thing was, he had very little clothing in the closet and most of their money was spent at restaurants. Eating was one of Tina's hobbies and she didn't hold back with the money. She made sure Tarell had very little money in his pocket; however, she did buy him a cell phone but monitored his calls. She would always say to him, "Nobody is gonna take care of you like I will. I'm the only one that cares about you."

Although Tarell had become dependent on her to take care of him, he now had a son whom he loved and adored which, made it even harder for him to leave her. He knew that if he would ever decide to leave, Tina would make it her business for him not to be able to see his son again.

Chapter Twenty-Four

Tarell's biggest fear was that if he left, his son would feel that he had abandoned him, just as Tarell felt his parents did with him. So more than anything, Tarell felt that he had to stay around for his son but hated the fact that he had no say so when it came down to him. He got mad when Tina's teenage sons would beat on Tarell Jr., and he couldn't say anything about it. When he did say something, Tina would get on him and threaten to put him out of the house. One day, little Tarell cried to his father after being thrown to the ground hard by his brother, Carl.

Tarell jumped up to discipline his stepson. Tina jumped in the middle and said, "I wish you would hit my son."

"Well, your son threw my son off the bed and hurt him."

Tarell's anger grew.

"He'll be alright; he's a boy and that's his brother," she said, raising her voice.

"As long as you are in my house, you'd better not

ever raise your hands to my kids or even look at them in any kind of way."

Tarell was angry. When it came down to someone hurting people he loved, like his son and even his biological mother, he would normally lose it, but this time, he didn't. Even with Tarell huffing, puffing and breathing hard, he just held his son and comforted him. The bullying administrated by Tina's sons towards little Tarell didn't stop, and all Tarell could do was witness the abuse. Inside, it made him angrier and angrier.

Chapter Twenty Five

Before going to prison and after hearing Tina was HIV positive, Tarell had started using condoms, just as he always did with Debbie and the other women he had been with. However, it didn't take Tina long before she convinced him not to use them. At first, she was all for it when they talked that day in the hospital when little Tarell was born.

After his release from prison, and while in bed with Tina that first night after having sex, she said, "Tarell, I don't want you wearing those condoms anymore. I don't like the way they feel."

"I don't want to catch AIDS," said Tarell.

Stroking his head and running her fingers through his hair, she said, "It's not AIDS; it's HIV, and as long as I take my medication, I can live a long life. I refuse to live the rest of my life with my husband wearing a condom every time we have sex," she continued.

"You're my husband, and husbands are not supposed to be having sex with their wives with condoms." Tina sat up, looked down at him and continued, "I don't believe you're insulting me like that! My own husband."

Tarell began to feel some kind of way and eventually ignored the idea of using a condom.

Chapter Twenty Six

After one year of being released from prison, Tarell finally got up enough courage to leave. Still miserable, confused, and depressed, he came across a guy on a street corner that was witnessing God's gospel to everyone who walked by. Tarell stopped to listen to the man.

"God loves you, son. Do you know that Jesus died for you?" asked the man.

"Yes," said Tarell.

"Are you OK, son? You look a little down."

"I'm okay," said Tarell unconvincingly.

The man sensed something wrong with Tarell and asked, "What is your name, son?"

"Tarell."

"Tarell, my name is Pete…Pete Haynes. I can see you have a lot on your mind and it is weighing heavy on your heart. You have to put it in God's hands son; it's too heavy for you to carry," said Pete.

He knew a lot was going on in Tarell's young life and he knew Tarell was disabled. He didn't even have to have a conversation with him because God had revealed it to Pete.

"Do you go to church?" he asked.

"No. I used to, but my wife does. She said I can't go with her."

"Oh, you're married?" Pete asked.

"Yes," said Tarell.

"You look so young! Well, too young to be married, but it's a good thing, marriage and looking young. How old are you?"

"22, but my wife is 47," said Tarell.

"So, your wife goes to church?"

"Yes," Tarell responded.

Pete didn't ask him why was he not able to go. God had revealed that to him as well. They continued to talk. During their conversation, Tarell shared some things with him about his past and present life.

"My heart goes out to you," said Pete. "God is with you. You hang in there, son."

"I will... I don't want to go back to my wife's house but my son lives there. When she gets mad, she always says she's gonna put me out her house. My real mother threw me out, my adoptive mother, my wife, and everyone else I've ever been with all put me out, and I hate it. It's not a good feeling."

After listening to Tarell, Pete pulled out a card with a lady minister's name and phone number on it and said, "Here, take this card and contact this minister. She has a big house and she takes in people that don't have a place to live."

As he handed Tarell the card, he continued, "Call this minister if you ever find yourself homeless and no place to go. She is a good friend of mine and she will take you in and help you. Her name is Theresa."

After three days of thinking about what Pete said, Tarell left Tina and everything behind. He went to the address on the card instead of calling. When he arrived at the address, he knocked on the door.

"Who is it?" A voice came from inside.

"My name is Tarell. I was talking to a man and he gave me this card and said I can come see you and that you will help me. He told me his name was Mr. Pete Haynes."

After hearing Pete's name, Theresa opened the door and said, "Oh, come in!"

"Thank you," Tarell said as he walked in.

Theresa was a light skinned, 46-year-old woman, who was 5 foot 3 and 135 pounds. She had shoulder-length hair and was very pretty. Theresa didn't look her age; she looked as though she was in her early thirties, but when she spoke, you could tell she was a lot older than that.

"Have a seat; you look nervous," Theresa said. She continued, "You said your name is Tarell?"

"Yes, that's the name my mother gave me, but my adoptive mother changed it to Jermaine. I don't like the name Jermaine so I use Tarell."

"Oh, I see. Well, my name is Theresa. What brings you by, Tarell?"

"I don't have no place to live, and I was wondering if you have a room for me to stay in."

"Well, I do have one room available. Where are you coming from?"

"I was living with my wife, but I can't stay there no more," Tarell said as he shifted nervously on the couch. While listening to Tarell and judging his character, Theresa sensed that he had a disability. Tarell continued, "She put me out, and when I'm there she always threatens to put me out, but I hate it there. I don't want to be there."

"Did you leave or did your wife put you out?"

"Well, I told her I was leaving, and she told me to get out after I said that. Even if I would have changed my mind, she still would have made me leave for saying it, but I wasn't gonna change my mind."

"Tarell, you and your wife need to try and work things out."

Theresa said this because she was a Christian woman. She felt that when it came to marriage, one must be very careful when interfering with someone else's. Her belief was that once a man and woman got married, they should at least try to do whatever it takes to stay together.

In Tarell's desperate state of mind, he said, "Please, Ms. Theresa, can I please stay here? I don't have no money to pay you, but if I have to, I'll get some from somewhere somehow."

Theresa sensed his desperation and said, "No, no, no, that's not the issue. Did you tell your wife you were taking a room somewhere else, and she was in agreement with it?"

"Yes, she is."

"Do you mind if I speak with her?"

"No, I'll call her,"

He took out his phone and started dialing. Tina answered after she recognized his number on her phone. When she answered, Tarell had his phone on speaker.

"What, Tarell!"

"I'm at a lady named Theresa's house and she is a minister that is going to let me stay at her house and she wanted to speak with you."

"About what?"

"She wanna know if you're in agreement with me staying at her house."

Because Tina was tired of Tarell for the time being she said, "I don't care where you stay; you're not coming back in here. So yes I'm in agreement with you staying there."

"Hold on," Tarell said as he handed Theresa the phone so that she could hear what his wife had said.

"Hi, my name is Theresa. Tarell tells me he has no place to go."

"He don't," Tina said, raising her voice a notch. "He can't stay at my house, and if you're gonna let him stay there then I'm in agreement, or if not then he'll just have to go to a shelter. If he's gonna stay there, make sure he calls his probation officer today and let her know where he's staying." Tina then hung up the phone before Theresa could respond.

Theresa shook her head in disgust, "You can stay in the room down the hall. Your wife mentioned that you were on probation."

"Yeah, I was arrested for sleeping with a girl that was sixteen years old. I was nineteen, but I didn't know what I did was wrong at the time. I went to jail for one year. Now I know what it's like to be in jail and it's no fun."

"What is your probation officer's name and number?" Theresa asked as she passed his phone back to him.

Tarell dialed his probation officer's number and spoke with the receptionist.

"Hi, can I speak with parole officer Gray?"

"Hold on a minute," said the receptionist.

"Parole officer Gray, can I help you?"

"Hi, Ms. Gray. This is Jermaine. I have somebody who wants to speak with you." Tarell handed the phone to Theresa.

"Hello, Ms. Gray; my name is Theresa Smith. Jermaine landed on my doorsteps with no place to go. I don't know if his wife put him out or he left—that's not clear—but I just needed to inform you of his whereabouts."

"Well, Ms. Smith, Jermaine can't just up and leave like that without someone coming out to your house. What town do you live in," she asked.

"West Haven."

"Oh, well that's not even our district. I would have to do a transfer from this town to your town's probation and that takes something like two weeks. Before he can stay there, your house needs to be approved. I'll put the transfer in Monday, but in the meantime he has to go back to his wife's house."

"Oh, okay; I'll let him know," said Theresa as she hung up the phone and handed it back to Tarell. "Your probation officer won't allow you to stay here until she puts in for a transfer and someone comes out to the house."

"But I don't have any place to go," he said with a worried look on his face.

"Your wife is gonna have to let you stay there until your probation say it's okay for you to stay here."

"She's not gonna let me stay there."

"She has to Tarell. It's the law."

"But I don't want to stay there. Please don't make me go back there," Tarell said, almost on the verge of tears.

Theresa got up and walked across the room because she couldn't look at Tarell without feeling sorry for him.

"There's nothing I can do, Tarell. Your probation officer said you have to. Call her back; let me see what I can do."

Tarell dialed his probation officer's number again and gave the phone to Theresa.

After the receptionist connected the call, Ms. Gray answered.

"Parole Officer Gray speaking."

"Hi, Ms. Gray, This is Theresa Smith; I just spoke with you concerning Jermaine."

"Yes, Ms. Smith."

"I just wanted to inform you that before Jermaine called you ten minutes ago, I had spoken with his wife who is refusing to let him go back home," said Theresa. "She doesn't want him there and apparently because of the way he says she treats him, he doesn't want to go back."

"He has to go back, and he has to go back today. All I can do is try and put a rush on the transfer so that it won't take two weeks."

"But if his wife is refusing to let him go back there, then what?" asked Theresa.

"She can't refuse to let him stay there, Ms. Smith; that's where he's been staying, so if she wants him out, then she will have to take the proper channels in doing so. Now if he's causing disruption at her house then that's another story."

"Ok, I hear what you're saying, but if it's okay with you, could he stay at my house until tomorrow? It wouldn't be as if he's establishing residency, it will be as though he only stayed the night. I'm asking this because I see his frustration and also in speaking with his wife, I heard hers as well. Tomorrow is another day, but today I think it really would be good for the both of them if he stayed here tonight."

"Okay," said Ms. Gray, "but I want him back at his wife's address tomorrow evening."

"Okay, I'll let him know. Thank you," Therese said as she hung up the phone.

Ms. Gray could have easily shut Theresa down and not heard what she had to say after already stating her position. However, Ms. Gray was a decent person and it wasn't just about her job. Theresa gave the phone back to Tarell and said, "She said you can stay today, but you have to go back to your wife's house tomorrow."

Tarell began to feel a little sense of relief, but then

he thought about how he would still be in the same position tomorrow when he would have to return.

"I can't go back there, not even tomorrow," said Tarell. "Please God; don't make me go back there! Ms. Theresa, you're a minister; please pray with me, please!"

Theresa saw how upset Tarell was after telling him he had to return to his wife's house. She took his hand, held it out and before she could say anything, Tarell began praying from the depths of his soul. As he squeezed her hands, he prayed.

"Lord, please allow me to stay at this house. I don't wanna go back to my wife's house. Please, Father in Heaven, hear my prayer. I'm not mad at my wife, but I don't want to be there. Help my wife and look out for my son. In Jesus' name, amen. Ms. Theresa, do you think God is gonna answer my prayer?"

Theresa held his hand tight and said, "Don't doubt it, just believe." Theresa released his hand and turned to go in the kitchen.

Chapter Twenty Seven

One of the guys who lived in the house came in from work and saw Theresa and Tarell.

"Hi Maurice, this is Tarell." Theresa said with a smile. "Tarell, this is Maurice. Maurice, Tarell is gonna be staying here with us."

Maurice held his hand out, greeted Tarell with a handshake, and said, "Good to meet you, Tarell"

"It's good to meet you too, sir," Tarell said as they shook hands.

"Call me Maurice."

"You'll meet the other guys as well, Tarell," Theresa said.

Some of them are still at work and some don't work because they are disabled. Other than my two teenage sons, Darren, who's eighteen and Kenneth, who is nineteen, there are five other guys here. When one leaves, another comes. They stay as long as they need to stay. All of the residents here are decent people, but some have been through a lot and some are still going through some stuff, just like yourself, and being here, they experience peace of mind. This is a house of peace," Theresa said proudly.

Tarell smiled and said, "I need some peace; one of my medicines that I take is to stop my mind from racing."

Theresa patted him on the shoulder and said, "You'll be alright. You have to try to think about all the good things. Think about all the good things that are happening for you now. Right now, in this moment."

Tarell started thinking about the things that was happening for him in that moment and said, "I feel happy in this moment" as he smiled.

"See, if you think of happy things, you'll be happy. You thought about what is happening in this moment and it made you happy," smiled Theresa. "Don't worry about tomorrow. When we prayed, we left it up to God to work out. Be happy in this day for what God has just done for you today."

"I pray that joy also be in you, because once you have joy, nobody can take it away. And that's when you can experience peace, and when you have peace, you won't worry," Theresa said with confidence.

"Well, that's what I want because I'm tired of worrying about things. I worry a lot," interjected Tarell.

"Oh, is that where those gray strands in your head come from? You're too young for that," said Theresa.

Tarell laughed and said, "You can see them? I only have like one or two."

"I'm just joking with you," Theresa said.

"Yeah, but I do have like one or two that are right in the front."

Theresa laughed and said, "Let's look at it as wisdom."

"Huh?" Tarell was confused.

"Nothing. Let me show you to your room," Theresa said, then turned to walk down the hall.

Tarell followed behind Theresa as she led him to his room. When Tarell saw his room, he said, "Wow, this is cool; my own room, with my own bed and TV! I always shared a room with the other kids in Ms. Thomas' house when I was living there, and then when I would stay with all those women, I had to share the room and bed with them. I had my own room for a little while when I was at Cashmere's house, but I didn't feel comfortable there. It was a lot of things going on in his house. Wow, this is cool! Thank you, Ms. Theresa."

"You're welcome," Theresa said as she turned and walked away. Looking over her shoulder, she said, "When you settle in or sometime later, we need to sit down so I can go over the house rules with you."

"Okay, I'll come in there in a minute."

"Take your time," she said.

Chapter Twenty Eight

An hour later, Tarell came into the kitchen where Theresa stood cooking over the stove. The kitchen was where she spent most of her time when she was home. Theresa was always cooking something because she loved to cook and had started a catering business out of her home. She only catered food on the weekends, and sold the food to different businesses. Tarell came in.

"I'm ready to go over the house rules, Ms. Theresa."

"Okay, let me get my rule book. You know every house should have rules and the people in the house must obey them. Rules are not made to be something hard but something used to simply keep everything in order," Theresa explained.

"However, before we get started, you may call me Theresa just as everyone else does. In here, everybody is called by his or her first name, including me, and no one is referred to as a tenant. This is a home and in this home everyone is looked on to be a part of this house. We are all family."

Theresa got up to get her rulebook and continued,

"We are friends to each other, not landlord and tenants. We all contribute to the bills so everyone in here is looked on to be an equal. It's just that God have placed me in charge and has given me rules to read to you all. In other words, this is your home and you have to treat it like your home."

"Okay, I understand," said Tarell.

Theresa then began to read off the house rules. "Rule number one: You must keep your room clean. Rule number two: everyone must clean up behind himself or herself when using the bathroom. For example, if you spill mouthwash on the sink or floor, you must clean it up. Rule number three: No women in the rooms. Rule number four: No overnight company."

The list went on. After going over everything, she said, "On the weekends, we have bible study and prayer for all those that care to join in. We have discussions on things dealing with life; a lot of the discussions would be talks pertaining to situations that the guys here have been through and are presently going through. Then we see what the bible has to say about it. You know, God always has the last word. At the end of the day, it's what He says that matters. The discussions are always interesting, and before leaving the kitchen table, everyone would leave learning something new. Sundays are church days. I don't force anyone to go. but the door is open to anyone that wants to."

Tarell was happy to hear that. By him being raised with Ms.Thomas, he always went to church and he loved it.

"Oh, I wanna go to church," he said happily. "I could never go when I was with my wife."

"Why?"

"Because she said that she didn't want me to embarrass her."

"You're welcome to come to church anytime you'd like, Tarell."

"Okay, that will be good. I would like to go every time you go."

"That's okay with me; church starts at eleven."

"Ok, I'll be ready. I use to go with my adoptive mother, Ms. Thomas, but that was a long time ago," he continued.

Chapter Twenty Nine

A s time went by that day, Tarell shared alot of things with Theresa. Theresa's heart was so overwhelmed by his story and she took helping him personal. She has a mentally disabled son who happened to be born on the same day as Tarell, but in a different year. Whereas Tarell was born July 22, 1984, Theresa's son Bryan was born July 22, 1979.

Her son had left home five years prior to the time Tarell showed up. She hadn't seen him since, but he would call twice a year to say that he was okay. Bryan was 22 when he left home. He was the same age as Tarell, but was now 27. Theresa thought about how Tarell landed on her steps and how she had *one* empty room available and no one even on the waiting list. She thought, *this is no coincidence; this could only be God.* Out of the love Theresa has for her son and knowing he was mentally challenged, she did what most mothers would do that has a disabled child. She sheltered him and was overly protective of him. She did just about everything for him, except teach him.

When her son became a teenager, people would often tell her that she needed to enroll him into a program where they would teach him some life skills, so that in the event of something happening to her, he would be able to take care of himself. But being a mother who felt she would always be around to take care of him, she neglected to do that. After hearing the family talking about it, Theresa's son would often tell her that he would like to go to a program for life skills, but it wasn't in her to do it. Even with her son being mentally challenged, what he wanted most, like every other disabled child, was to live a normal life. He wanted to learn to do things for himself. Theresa failed to realize this until it was too late. Her son just simply got up one day and left.

Chapter Thirty

It was easy to see why Theresa would take helping Tarell so personal. Her agenda was to do with him what she neglected to do with her own son—teach him. She felt God was giving her a second chance, and it brought healing to her to help someone with a great need.

Tarell, like Theresa's son, was very intelligent when it came down to things dealing with science and computers, and they could also remember things that had taken place many years ago as if they had a computer chip installed in their head.

The problem was that their life skills needed to be developed, and it was a problem that could be resolved. The solution was simply to just make some time and teach them. Unlike other children that would see things and pick them up, it takes a lot more work and time with a mentally challenged individual. Both boys had an IQ below 70 and could only be taught up to a sixth grade level, but with adequate guidance, they could live and work independently and productively as adults. Cooking for themselves or doing their own laundry, handling money, or food shopping were life events that they'd have to be taught.

Being a woman of God, and a woman that trusts God, Theresa knew that wherever her son was, he was in God's hands and care.

Chapter Thirty One

The next day, Theresa got up early to attend a gospel festival. Tarell and a few of the guys in the house that weren't working that day also came along. Theresa rented a vender booth and decided to sell some things she had put together. Theresa had a gift with words and had written over 300 inspirational sayings. She put the sayings on wall plaques, t-shirts, women's handbags, and bumper stickers. Theresa was all about getting God's message out there, and God was assisting her in doing so. Everybody that came along lent a hand and assisted her in selling all her items.

Later that day, while at the festival, she told Tarell to call his wife so that he could let her know what the probation officer said. He didn't want to call her because he didn't want to go back, but he agreed to call anyway because he knew that Tina wouldn't let him come back, even after the probation officer instructed him to. Tarell walked away from the booth to a quiet area and dialed Tina's number.

She answered on the fifth ring, just when Tarell

was about to hang up. "Yeah, what do you want?" Tina said, recognizing his number on her caller I.D.

"It's me, Tarell."

"What do you want? Why are you calling me after just one day? What, you can't make it without me?" Tina spat.

"My probation officer said that I have to come back there."

"Oh no, you're not!" Tina said, growing angry at the thought of Tarell coming back to her house.

"I can't stay at Ms. Theresa's house," Tarell said after hearing Tina's attitude.

Theresa walked over in time to hear what Tina was saying and interjected. "She has to let you back in the house, Tarell, but since she's saying that she won't, then let me talk to her."

Tarell handed Theresa the phone.

"Hello, this is Theresa. I spoke with the probation officer yesterday and she said he has to come back there until he gets approved to stay elsewhere. She's going to do a transfer on Monday, but it will take approximately two weeks to go through."

Tina wasn't interested in what Theresa had to say, but asked, "Where do you live, and why does she have to do a transfer?"

"I live on Andrew Street in West Haven. She only agreed to him being out of your house for one night, but said he has to return back there tonight," Theresa explained.

"No! He's not coming back here," Tina said with an attitude.

"Where is he going to go?" inquired Theresa.

"I don't care where he goes," Tina barked back.

"Well, it's not like he can go anywhere; his probation officer said he has to return to your house." Theresa began to get a little aggravated. "Listen, I hate that all this is happening," she continued, "but he landed on my doorstep, and I can't just put him out knowing you're not gonna take him in or knowing he doesn't have a place to go. He is disabled and he doesn't need to be out there in those streets or even in a men's shelter."

"Well, they have a lot of disabled men in shelters. That's what the shelters are for...homeless people, disabled or not. The way I see it, if he can't stay at your house, "*Ms.*," then that makes him homeless." Tina continued, "And now that you see he has mental problems, you need to make sure he's taking his medication. I did take the time to call his nurse to let her know he was no longer at my house, so she's going to be calling him to get your address."

Disliking the way that Tina called her "Ms.," Theresa said, "My name is Theresa or you can call me Ms. Smith... and a nurse already came by the house this morning."

Theresa didn't have a problem with Tina calling her Ms., but it was just the way she said it.

"Well, I have to go; my battery is dying." The phone cut off, and for the rest of that evening, neither Tarell nor Theresa could get in touch with her.

Chapter Thirty Two

The next morning, Theresa called Tina, and she picked up the phone on the first ring.

"Good morning, this is Theresa; we got disconnected yesterday, but as I was saying, Tarell's probation officer said he needed to go back to your house as of last night."

"Yeah, I heard you yesterday," Tina said, still very rude. "And I remember telling you he can't come back here."

"He doesn't have any clothing besides what he had on when he arrived at my house," said Theresa. "That was two days ago. And he doesn't have any money to buy anything, either. I don't have much money, but I gave him enough to get him some underclothing."

"He gets money on the first of every month, but when he got his check last week, I had to buy me a car because mine broke down, so he's just gonna have to make the best of what he has," Tina said.

Theresa started to feel herself getting angry at Tina's sarcasm, but she was not the type of person to catch these kinds of feelings, so she didn't feed into it.

Instead of retaliating, she just said, "He mentioned that he receives food stamps on a card from state welfare and that his food stamps came on the card yesterday. Although he's not able to contribute anything, it would help if he had his card so that he can purchase some food for himself."

"Well, I just used the money yesterday," said Tina. "I filled my house with food, but if you want I will buy enough packs of Oodles of Noodles to last him for the rest of the month."

Theresa was disgusted with Tina's conduct and began to understand why Tarell didn't want to go back there, but held her thoughts and simply responded, "Oodles of Noodles?"

"Or I'll give him the twenty dollars in food stamps that's left over on the card and he can get them himself; they only cost fifteen cents a pack so twenty dollars is more than enough," she continued.

Theresa wanted to hang the phone up in her face, but being a woman of God, she knew just how to deal with people like Tina.

"Thank you, but that's okay; you just keep the Oodles and Noodles and/or the twenty dollars. But, besides all that, Tarell still has to return to your house for a couple of weeks, maybe less."

"Listen *Ms.*; don't bring him to my house. I already spoke to the police and they said I don't have to take him back," Tina said with threat in her voice.

"I can't see the police telling you that. It's the law that if someone has established residency, you can't put them out just like that. Even if they leave for a day or two, all of Tarell's stuff is still there," said Theresa.

"*Ms.*, I really don't have time for this. I have to go." Tina hung up the phone in Theresa's face.

It was Sunday morning and Theresa really didn't want to start it off by hearing all the hateful things Tina was saying. She definitely wasn't going to feed into them by telling her off, especially when Tina purposely kept calling her "Ms." in that disrespectful tone.

After hanging up the phone, Theresa, Darren, Kenneth, Faze, Tarell and Maurice got dressed and went to church. Later that day, Curtis, who also lived in the house, Tarell, and Maurice were sitting on the porch talking and laughing when Tina pulled up in front of the house, blowing her horn like a crazy woman. Since there was only one Andrew Street in the town, and it was a dead end street, it wasn't hard for Tina to find Theresa's house. Tina's type of behavior was unusual in this quiet suburban neighborhood. Theresa didn't need all this commotion around her house. She could hear Tina from her kitchen as she went to the front door to see what was going on.

Tina yelled out her driver's side window at Tarell saying, "Come get your clothes!" She threw them out the window. Tarell could see her two sons in the car as he went to pick his clothes up off the ground.

Theresa came out to the porch, walked down a couple of steps and said, "Why are you coming over here with his clothes, throwing them all out in the street and making all this noise? He has to go back to your house and you're going to let him in. If you don't take him home with you now, then I'll bring him there myself, and then you can call that cop you said you spoke to so he can tell me that Tarell can't stay there. If he could stay here then I would let him, but I'm not trying to get him *or* myself into trouble by going against what his probation officer said!"

Theresa went along and did her part. She pursued Tarell's going home like she was supposed to do. She knew it was God's will for her to pursue it, and out of obedience she did; but even so, she knew that God had a bigger plan for Tarell's life. Theresa was one that knew she had to respect one in higher authority, even the probation officer who God had allowed to be in her position and have the upper hand in this matter.

Still picking up his clothes from the ground, Tina pulled off without responding to what Theresa said.

As Tarell headed back to the porch, Maurice said, "What was that all about? Who was that lady?"

"My wife," Tarell said with great embarrassment in his tone.

"Your wife?" Maurice and Curtis said simultaneously.

"Wow... She's a big girl," said Curtis.

"Yeah, she is," Tarell said as he laughed it off.

Maurice was also married and going through some stuff with his wife. Maurice worked a lot, and his wife would always complain about him not spending any time with her, so she eventually started cheating on him with her ex- boyfriend.

Up until the day that Maurice moved out of his house, his wife continued messing around with her ex-boyfriend. She even brought him into their home while Maurice was at work, and she made it no secret as the guy would just simply get up and leave when Maurice came through the door. But it didn't take Maurice's wife long before she realized that she had made a big mistake and wanted Maurice back. Maurice was a decent man, but the thing was, he couldn't see anything wrong with him working all the time. He felt that as long as he was bringing in the money to pay the bills, it was OK. Eventually, he did end up going back to his wife and saw his fault in it as well.

Within fifteen minutes, Tina was back in front of Theresa's house, yelling.

"You know what, Tarell? You can come back home, but you're sleeping in the basement and don't even think about coming out of it. That's where you'll be staying until your transfer is done!"

She pulled off.

"You said your wife is a Christian?" Theresa asked.

"Yeah, she goes to church a lot."

"How is the basement, Tarell?"

"I hate it down there; it has spiders down there and it's no bed down there," said Tarell.

Theresa didn't say anything.

"Please don't take me back to her house.

She's gonna treat me real bad, I know she is," he continued.

Tarell was almost in tears as fear flooded his eyes.

Theresa called his probation officer to tell her what had taken place. Ms. Gray picked up after the fourth ring and said, "Hello?"

"Hi, this is Theresa Smith, I spoke with you on Friday concerning Jermaine? I'm sorry to be calling you on a Sunday, but Jermaine said I could reach you at this number."

"Oh, it's OK; it's my cell phone number. Did Jermaine go back to his wife's house?"

"No, me and Jermaine both tried to make contact with her all evening yesterday, but she didn't pick up her phone, then when we went by her house, we got no answer. Jermaine spoke to her earlier yesterday around 3pm and told her what you said about him going back there yesterday, but she gave him a hard time. I tried to talk to her but she told me not to bring him there, and then we were disconnected."

After that, Theresa filled Ms. Gray in on the latest stuff that had just taken place that Sunday pertaining to Tina and her behavior.

After explaining to Officer Gray what had happened, Theresa said, "I'm a minister and have been housing people in need for some years now; some are working people, and some are disabled. The ones that can contribute to the house expenses contribute, but then there are people that need a place to stay and have no income. I'm telling you all this because after speaking to his wife and hearing all that was said and seeing her actions, I really don't think it's in Jermaine's best interest to be there at his wife's house, not even for the time it will take for the transfer to go through."

Ms. Gray was silent for a minute and knew what Theresa was talking about. She had witnessed the abuse Tina inflicted on Tarell and the controlling attitude she had towards him when she would accompany him during his probation visits. She also knew that this wasn't the first time Tina had put him out of the house.

After Theresa finished speaking, Ms. Gray said, "He's not a bad kid; he does everything he's supposed to do while being on probation." He had no prior record before the rape charge. It was just an unfortunate thing that happened to him. However, if you're willing to take him in then it's okay with me. I'll do the transfer tomorrow, and I'll contact the probation office in your town to let them know the situation."

"Okay," said Theresa.

"Thank you, Ms. Smith for all of your help with Jermaine. Being at your house will be good for him."

"You're welcome, and I thank you as well," Theresa said before hanging up the phone.

After getting off the phone, she turned to Tarell and said, "Good news, Tarell; your probation officer said you can stay here at the house. She's going to take care of the transfer tomorrow."

Tarell was happy to hear the news.

"Thank you, Theresa!" He looked up at the ceiling

with joy in his eyes. "Thank you, God! God answered my prayer. You said to believe, and I did, and He answered my prayer."

Tarell was so overwhelmed and full of gratitude.

"Anything that needs to be done around here, I'll do it. I'll wash the dishes everyday and clean up whatever needs to be cleaned, and I'll make sure the trash is taken out."

"You don't have to do all that, Tarell."

"It's okay; I want to, Theresa. Pleaseee. I know how to clean; I always did it when I was at my wife's house,"

"Tarell, I know where you're coming from. It's a good feeling when you get something that you wanted so bad, something you prayed for and God gave it to you. You become so happy that you just want to do something to show your appreciation. God knows you appreciate what He did, and it's good that you want to show it. However, if you clean up everything everyday, then there won't be anything left for the people around here to do, so let's all pitch in and that way we all can show God how much we appreciate the things He did for us. You can take the trash out; that can be your job."

"Okay, and I'll help sometimes with the dishes. I can wash dishes good; I mix the dish liquid with some bleach and the dishes come out real clean."

"Okay, that will be fine. My grandmother used to put a little bleach in her dish water as well," said Theresa.

Tarell's phone started ringing, and he answered

it on speaker, as he often did. It was Tina, and as soon as Tarell answered, she began yelling.

"You know what? After thinking about it, I changed my mind; you can't stay in the basement either."

She hung up. Tarell didn't even bother to call her back to tell her he didn't need to. He just put his phone in his pocket and laughed.

Chapter Thirty Three

Tarell was so overjoyed that he took the garbage out, and when he saw Theresa cleaning the bathroom, he offered to clean the tub.

"Tarell, I have it."

"No, Theresa, I'll do it. It's gonna come out real clean," he said as he got the cleaner and got on his knees to start cleaning the tub. "I was the one who kept the bathroom the cleanest at my wife's house. Now her sons will have to do it, but they're lazy. They're not gonna help her; she's not gonna have nobody to help her."

He paused, then continued, "They be leaving their clothes on the bathroom floor when they come out the shower and they don't even lift the toilet seat up when they use the bathroom. They be telling Tina that it be me who leaves it up. Boy, am I glad to be gone from there." Then he paused again and said, "It's just too bad that Tina has to do all the cleaning by herself now. I'm glad to be gone, but I keep thinking about my son. Do you think she will let me see him?"

"She should. I'm sure your son misses you as well and would like to see you, too."

"I'm gonna call her tomorrow and ask her if I can see my son," Tarell said.

Tarell may not have been taught a lot of things, but he was taught how to clean. Theresa noticed that he was very good at cleaning and took pride in his work.

"Tarell, I remember your wife from way back. I'm talking back like twenty years ago."

"You knew my wife twenty years ago?"

"I knew *of* her; we weren't friends, but I used to see her around."

Back then, Theresa was into the streets and had heard rumors about Tina, but she never gave it any thought as to whether there was any truth in the rumors. Theresa wasn't into all the gossip, but being in the streets, you can't help but hear things, even when you don't want to. In the streets, people talk, and sometimes it was hard to ignore; especially when it was "juicy gossip."

People talked about how Tina was in a relationship with a guy who was very controlling and often ran around on her. They talked about how she was being used and how guys were always using her for her money and a place to live. Then, ten years ago, right before Theresa left the streets alone, there had been rumors that Tina, who was in her thirties, was in a relationship with a man that was in his fifties. People talked about how she was crazy over this man, but he treated her badly. They said he was mean to her and very controlling, and made her do things against her will. It was said that he preyed on women who were weak with low self -esteem, and he was known to mess with prostitutes. They said these were the kind of men Tina always attracted, although, she was a decent woman. They were men who controlled her. Now, the shoe was on the other foot, and she was finally the one in control.

Theresa continued to speak to Tarell and told him, "It appears that she does care about you, at least enough to not want to see you in the streets. She acts tough, but she's really not as tough and mean as she wants people to believe she is. As tough as she tries to be, I believe she's content knowing that you are safe. What I'm trying to say is, I think she's glad that you are here and not on the streets. I did sense that she had some concern with certain things that pertained to you. She wanted to make sure you contacted your probation officer. I don't believe she wanted to see you get in any trouble, even if she is acting like she doesn't care and gave us a hard time about you going back there."

"Huh?" Tarell said, not understanding what Theresa was talking about.

Theresa sensed his confusion and continued, "Being in a relationship with someone and being around them every day, most times, you develop feelings for that person. Even when things don't go right, or if you weren't in love from the start, or even if it's not an "in love" thing, and... even when you're being mistreated, you still want that other person to be well. You still care. Just like you being glad that you are not there at her house any more, you were also saying just a moment ago how she's not gonna have nobody to help her clean because her sons were lazy. You said it with some concern in feeling a little bad for her. So, although you don't want to be there, you care enough by thinking about who's going to help her. It's a natural thing to still care, even if you don't want to be there or someone doesn't want you there."

"Oh, I understand what you're saying. You mean because she's my wife and I'm her husband, even though I'm not in love with her, its okay for me to care about her?"

"Yes, that's exactly what I'm saying," Theresa said.

"And you said she probably care about me, that's why she said she's okay with me staying at your house."

"Yes."

"Oh," Tarell responded.

Theresa said all of this because she wanted Tarell to know that it's OK to care about someone, even when you're not in love with them. As Theresa spoke to Tarell, she thought to herself.

When one cares, it shows proof of love, and its God's will to love as how God loves us. And if we have God's love in us, as she sees Tarell does, then it is a natural thing—a God thing—for one to still care about the person, no matter what the person does or has done. Just like God, we care about people we love, and we love the people we care about... This includes even those that we look at as an "enemy."

Chapter Thirty Four

The next morning, Tarell woke up and went to the kitchen where Theresa was and said, "Good morning. You cooking breakfast; do you need help?'

"Good morning, Tarell. Yes, I'm cooking breakfast and I am just about done, but you can watch me cook the eggs if you'd like. I learned a lot hanging around the kitchen watching my mother cook."

"Ok."

Tarell stayed in the kitchen watching Theresa cook.

"My nurse is on her way to give me my medication, and my probation officer called me and said she's gonna stop by this afternoon to check the house."

"Oh, okay. That's good," Theresa said.

"She told me that if I go back to my wife's house, she's gonna violate me, but she said she was only playing."

Theresa half laughed. "She was saying that she don't want you going back," she clarified.

"Yeah, I know; that's what she said. I spoke with my adoptive mother this morning and I told her I don't live with my wife anymore and she was happy. She told me not to go back to her house because she's only using me."

Theresa continued to cook as she listened to Tarell talk.

"I call her once in a while. I don't ever speak to my adoptive sisters and brothers or my adoptive cousins or other family members because everybody is adults now and some are married. My adoptive mother said they have their own lives now, but she says everyone is okay. I try to call my adoptive brother Robert sometimes, but he's always busy. He tells me he's gonna call me back but he don't. He has an African wife and a baby."

Tarell began to feel sad. "Robert is Ms. Thomas' real son. She has two real sons and she had a real daughter that died before she adopted me and my adoptive sister Lisa. She had other foster kids, too."

Ms. Thomas had just recently revealed all this to Tarell. Up until she revealed it, he didn't know whether the other kids he called his siblings was adopted as well.

"How many foster kids did she have?" asked Theresa.

"Probably like twenty all together, but some stayed for a short time and some stayed longer. She treated all of us the same, but her real kids were treated just a little bit better than us.

"She was mean to us; she treated us badly. I think she feels real bad about the way she treated me and now she's an old lady, that's why she talks to me when I call. I didn't call her for a long time, but I always remembered her number. Now, she act like she loves me but she don't."

"So you think she's just telling you that?" Theresa asked.

"Yeah, cause I gave her my phone number, but she never calls me; she say she be busy. But she always tells me before I hang up with her that she loves me, but she never told me that before when I lived with her. When my wife put me out the first time, I called her and asked her if I can go back to her house, but she said no, and that she didn't have any room for me."

"Well, sounds like she made some mistakes. Everybody makes mistakes, Tarell. Even when people love you, sometimes they have a funny way of showing it; sometimes people just don't know how to show it. Tarell, you have to look at the good things," said Theresa. "She gave you a place to stay and clothed you, even if it wasn't with the clothes you wanted, and she fed you."

Theresa was always trying to look at the good in every situation and not focus so much on the bad; she felt that no matter how bad things looked, whatever the situation, we must always see God in it.

"Yeah, I know you're right. She did do those things," said Tarell.

"Okay, so you have to be a little more grateful for the things she did do, and let God be the one concerned about what she didn't do. So in other words, Tarell, what I'm trying to say is, always remember the good things and try to forget about the bad things because God wants you to be happy, and if you're thinking about the bad things, it's only going to make you sad. When you're sad, He's sad."

Tarell listened carefully and had a serious look on his face.

Theresa continued, "Ms. Thomas must have taught you how to pray, because I can see you know how to pray as I listened to you the other day."

"Yeah, she did. She used to make us read the Bible and pray every day. I like to pray, but I don't understand the Bible."

"It's good you like to pray, and one day you will understand the Bible. Sometimes it just takes a little time, but you will understand it one day because God wants you to understand it. I didn't understand it for a long time myself, but God knew how much I wanted to understand it, and because He knew, He helped me. And because you want to understand it, He will help you, too."

Theresa continued to pray and read the Bible with Tarell every day. Although Tarell was mentally a child, Theresa didn't talk to him as such. She thought that doing that would hinder his growth, and since he was able to learn, her plan—which was God's plan— was to bring him up to a higher level, beyond the disability. When he didn't understand certain things, she would explain it to him in a way that he could. There are times when things have to be simplified for even "normal" adults.

While Theresa was in the kitchen serving the food, the doorbell rang. It was Tarell's nurse.

"Hi, Tarell," she said as she entered the front door. Tarell led her to the kitchen to introduce her to Theresa.

"Hi, I'm one of his nurses. My name is Ann."

"Hi," said Theresa.

"I'll be coming by every day," continued Ann.

"Oh okay," Theresa said. "I met one of the other nurses that had come by."

"Oh, that was Wanda. It's one more that you haven't met, but she's on vacation until next week. The three of us usually rotate shifts, but we come by twice a day to give Tarell his medication. Someone comes in the morning around this time, and then he gets his meds again at six in the evening."

"Oh, okay," Theresa said. "So, Tarell, you know you have to be around the house during those hours."

"Yeah, I will," said Tarell.

Days later, Theresa realized that Tarell wasn't a person that hung outside. He would only go outside when he saw Theresa going somewhere. Tarell followed Theresa everywhere. He would wake up out of his sleep if he heard her car starting up, and before she could pull off, he would run to the front door and yell, "Hold up, Theresa. Can I come?"

The only other times he would be outside were when the other guys in the house would be on the porch. Tarell got along well with the other guys in the house, but stuck close to Theresa as if he were her child. Tarell's nurse left after giving him his medicine.

Shortly afterwards, the phone rang. Theresa, looking at the caller ID, saw it was her husband Eric.

Eric was away on military duties. He had been in the military over twenty years and had been married to his wife for fifteen. He was fifty years old with a deep southern accent, and was very handsome. He was dark skinned, six foot two, 200 pounds, and was madly in love with his wife.

Theresa answered the phone excitedly. "Hi, Honey!"

"Hi, Sweetie Pie; how's my baby doing this morning?"

"Good."

"Busy morning?"

"No, not really; just got finish making breakfast. I have two appointments later this morning, but it shouldn't take too long." Her thoughts quickly shifted. "Remember when I told you I wanted you to meet somebody that moved in the other day, but he was sleep?"

"Yes, I remember," said Eric.

"His name is Tarell," she continued. "I have you on speaker; he's a good kid. Well, not kid, but young man. I say kid because being our age, you know how we tend to look at young people to be kids. Tarell, this is my husband Eric."

"Hi, Mr. Eric," said Tarell.

"Hi there! How are you? You don't have to call me Mr., just call me Eric."

"Okay, and I'm doing good. I just moved in the other day; my wife put me out of her house."

"Her house... isn't it your house too?"

"No, it's her house; I just used to live there. But she put me out and... well, I left because I was tired of being there."

"Oh, I see," said Eric.

"Theresa told me that you were in the military and that you will be coming home soon" said Tarell.

"Yeah, I'll be coming home in the next few months or so."

"Oh, while you're gone you don't have to worry about anything, because I'm gonna make sure the trash is taken outside, and I'll help Theresa do the dishes. I'm gonna do them whenever she don't feel like doing them."

"Oh, well thank you, Son."

"You're welcome. Well, I'm gonna go lay down now; my nurse just gave me my medicine and sometimes it makes me sleepy."

"Oh okay. What do you take medicine for?"

"I take it for depression and anxiety. I just be having a lot on my mind and I can't control my thoughts. The doctors said I have racing thoughts because I be thinking about too many things at a time. And some of the things make me depressed, mainly things about my real mother and father. I was adopted when I was a baby."

"Well, you can't let those things get to you. You have to try and think of more positive things."

"Yeah, I know. That's what Theresa said, but—"

Eric cut him off. "No, there are no buts. You can do it."

"I know, but—" Eric cut him off again.

"No... no; get the "but" out the way."

Tarell smiled and said, "Okay."

"Tarell, let me talk to Eric before he hangs up," said Theresa.

"Okay," Tarell responded. "Well it was good talking to you, Eric. I'm gonna go lay down now."

"Okay, it was good talking to you too." Tarell handed Theresa the phone and she took it off the speaker.

"Hey honey... you there?"

"Yeah, I'm here," Eric responded. "I didn't know that young man was disabled; you didn't mention that on the phone the other day."

"I know I didn't," Theresa responded.

Theresa didn't mention Tarell's disability to Eric because she knew what he was going to say.

"Honey, do you think you should be doing this? I know you still feel guilty about Bryan but there's nothing to feel guilty about. You did your best and you did a good job," he said.

"This is not about guilt, Eric. I have to help him. God has given me another chance to get it right. I will do for him what I didn't do for my own child. I will teach him everything he needs to know to take care of himself," she declared.

"Baby, listen to me; you don't have to do this!" Eric pleaded.

Eric was concerned that taking Tarell in might

be too much on Theresa. He felt that Tarell being there might remind her too much of Bryan.

"Eric, please—"

"Okay, Sweetie Pie. You know I'm with you in whatever you do. I love you," he said.

"I love you, too... and thank you." Theresa hung up the phone.

Although Bryan wasn't Eric's biological son, he loved him as if he was his own child. Along with Theresa's other children he had raised Bryan from the time since he was twelve. Theresa didn't have any children by Eric. Both, he and Theresa were in previous marriages that ended up in divorce before the two got together. Eric has two biological sons, but looked at all their children to be his.

When Eric hung up, he was in deep thought as he remembered that night that Bryan left and what had taken place. Theresa was in her bedroom with Eric, and she dropped to her knees as she wept painfully.

"Oh God!" she cried. "Oh God, my son... my son. I don't understand! What have I done? What did I do to deserve this... haven't I done all that you asked of me?" Theresa wept from the depths of her soul.

In all the years of Theresa and Eric's marriage, Eric had never seen his wife break down like that, and all Eric could do was get down on the floor beside her and comfort her. He held her with tears in his eyes.

The next day, Theresa spoke to Eric and said she heard a voice from Heaven.

"It said, '*It's not what you did, Theresa, it's what*

you didn't do.' The voice said, *'I'm more concerned about the things that you don't do than the things that you do. Your eyes are now opened,'* it said, *'don't be afraid, Theresa, I love you.'*

"In that moment, my eyes were opened and God showed me some things. He showed me how I was neglecting my son's needs. He showed me in a vision of flashbacks how Bryan came to me day after day, asking me to teach him how to do things like his laundry, and I ignored his request. I would say OK, but never did it. I made all kinds of excuses, all because I always did these things for him. He kept coming to me asking me to teach him how to do so many things that I realize today that he needed to learn. All those times he came to me and I kept ignoring his request, but he never gave up and he never stopped coming until the day he left. And I didn't see or even realize what I had done until God revealed it. All Bryan wanted was for me to teach him."

Seeing all of this was painful for Theresa. She began crying.

"I thought I was doing everything right by my son and by God, and I was afraid; but, God knew my motives were pure, and my intentions was good; but even so, I know that there are always consequences in everything. Even things we are not aware that we do."

Chapter Thirty Five

Almost two weeks passed since Tarell moved in. It was movie night at the house. One night out the week, anyone who wanted to would get together and watch movies in the living room. Then there were times when BBQ's took place during the summer months.

Tarell loved being at the house with the other guys and told them that this was the first time he ever felt like he was a part of a family. Every time he would do something wrong or forget to do something, he would always ask Theresa if she was going to put him out the house.

One evening, Tarell forgot to take the trash outside and Theresa called him to remind him about it before he went to bed. He came in the kitchen to take it out and said, "I'm sorry, I forgot. I won't forget again. Are you mad at me? Are you gonna make me leave?"

"No, why would I do that? I'm not going to make you leave. You are so used to being put out that you fear any little thing you do wrong, or forget to do, will result in you being put out," Theresa said. "I don't want you worrying about that, you hear me?"

"Yes," answered Tarell.

"I'm here to help you, and you will leave when you are ready to leave. But before you leave, I will make it my business to teach you the things you need to know to take care of yourself."

Tarell had a look of excitement on his face. "Are you gonna teach me how to cook?"

"Yes I am," Theresa answered.

"And how to do my own laundry?"

"Yes."

"And how to drive? Because I really want to learn how to drive so I can get my license."

"Yes, I'm going to teach you how to drive." She paused. "Well, I'm going to take you to register for driving school because they are better equipped to teach you than I am."

"Oh, okay, but Eric can just teach me when he comes home. I'll ask him when he calls tonight. I'd rather Eric teach me. It's a man's thing," he continued, a serious look now plastered across his face.

"Oh, well excuse me, said Theresa."

Tarell laughed and said, "I don't mean it like that. It's just that most times a father is the one that teaches his son how to drive."

"I got you," said Theresa, now smiling. Eric and Tarell had become very close. Eric was still away, but Tarell would speak to him every time he called. He would often talk to Eric about things that he only felt comfortable talking to an older male about. He looked at Eric like the father he never had. While on the phone one day and before ending their call, Tarell said to Eric, "I love you."

Eric responded with, "I love you too, son."

When Tarell hung up the phone, he felt good about what Eric had said to him.

"Did you hear that, Theresa? He said he loves me. He called me his son."

Tarell began to smile even more. "He said he loves me and I believe him."

Theresa smiled, and then said, "Eric loves you. He looks at you like you're his own son."

"Oh yeah, Theresa; I wanted to ask you if you can help me open a bank account. Could you show me how to open one?" Tarell asked.

"You should already have a bank account. You get an SSI check every month, the money don't go into an account?"

"No, I don't have an account; my money goes on this card." Tarell pulled the card out of his wallet to show it to Theresa.

"This card is linked to a bank account. You had to go into a bank to open an account at one point," she said.

"No, I never did. Maybe my wife did."

"Tarell, unless she knows someone at the bank, I don't see how she could have done that without you present. I'll take you to the bank tomorrow so that you can see that you already have an account. You can get a bankbook while you're there, so I can show you how to keep record of your account. I'm also going to show you how to fill out a deposit slip and a withdrawal slip." Tarell was smiling from ear to ear.

"The deposit slip will allow you to put money into the account, and the withdrawal slip will allow you to take money out," Theresa continued.

That next evening, Tarell called his adoptive mother, Ms. Thomas.

"Hello?"

"Hi, Mom."

"Hi, Jermaine. How are you doing?"

"Good; I'm still at the lady's house I was telling you about."

"That's good."

Before Ms. Thomas could say anything else, Tarell had already cut her off. "Hold on, Mom. Say hi to Theresa. Theresa, this is Ms. Thomas on the phone."

He handed Theresa the phone.

"Hello," Theresa said.

"Hi, how are you?" responded Ms. Thomas.

"Oh, I'm doing good and yourself?" inquired Theresa.

"I'm okay, just trying to hang in there," said a tired sounding Ms. Thomas.

Before Theresa could say another word, Tarell spoke. "Hold up Theresa, give me the phone for a minute." Theresa handed it to him.

"I want to put it on speaker." Tarell took the phone and put it on speaker, and then sat it on the kitchen table.

"Okay, Mom; I just put it on speaker. Mom, tell

Theresa how I used to sing in the church choir when I was little."

"Yeah, he used to sing in the choir," she repeated.

"Tell her how everybody used to clap when I sang."

"Yeah, they loved the way he sang. Jermaine has a beautiful voice."

"Mom, I used to sing on the trains and I used to make a lot of money. That's when I was living on the trains. I don't want to live back on the trains, but I'm thinking about going back on the trains so I can make more money."

"Don't you do that Jermaine! It's dangerous on those trains, do you hear me? Don't you do that," she demanded.

"I'm not. I was just joking. Mom, tell Theresa about the time when I made those sneakers out of rubber and cloth. Do you remember that, Mom?"

"Yes, I remember. You're a very gifted child." Tarell was smiling as Ms. Thomas spoke.

"Remember, Mom; I was trying to wear them outside and you wouldn't let me, but you let me wear them in the house."

"Yes, I remember."

"And remember how good I was at sports, and all the trophies I won?"

"Yes, I remember. I still have all the trophies and the pictures of you and your team."

"You do?" Tarell was very happy to hear that. "Can you send them to me?"

"I have to pull them out; I packed them up and put them away when I moved," explained Ms. Thomas.

"Mom, can you unpack them and send them to me so I can show people?"

"Yes, I'll send them when I get a chance. Theresa, are you still there?"

"Yes, I'm here, Ms. Thomas. I'm just listening to all the amazing things you're telling me about Jermaine."

"Yes, Jermaine is a special child with many gifts. He's a good person and he has a big heart. You won't have any problems out of him. He's been through a lot, but God is good."

"Amen," Theresa said. "Yes he is."

"Mom we be praying every night," said Tarell. "Sometimes, all the people in the house pray, and sometimes it be just me and Theresa."

"That's good, Jermaine. I want y'all to keep me in y'all prayers."

"Okay, mom; we will."

"We sure will, Ms. Thomas," said Theresa. "And you pray for us, too."

"I will, Sweetie. Jermaine I'm gonna hang up now. I love you."

"I love you. Too."

"I love you, Theresa, and thanks for everything," said Ms. Thomas.

"You're welcome, and I love you too. Jermaine will be okay; you take care of yourself."

Theresa sensed Ms. Thomas' concern for Tarell but she also sensed that Ms. Thomas knew he was in good hands. There was an apparent sense of guilt within Ms. Thomas, and being able to relate, she felt compassion for her.

After Ms. Thomas hung up, Theresa said, "She sounds like a very nice lady."

"Yeah, now she is, but she sounded like a different person on the phone just now. I mean, she's a nice lady now; she's always nice to me when I call her, but she still be cursing a lot. I didn't hear her say not one curse word this time, though. If you weren't listening, I'm sure some curse words would have come out her mouth."

Theresa laughed and said, "She used to curse?"

"No, not "used to." She still does. But she don't do it at church or around her friends."

"Oh, but she still sounds like a nice lady. She knows that she has some things not right with her, like perhaps cursing. That's why she asked us to pray for her," Theresa explained. "And we know we have some things that are not right with us, and that's why we need people to pray for us."

"She's a nice lady now, even though she still curses. But we will just pray for her when we pray," Tarell said.

Chapter Thirty Six

It had been almost one month since Tarell moved into the house. He had been getting along well, but missed his son a great deal. Tarell was trying hard not to let it get the best of him. Some days he was a little depressed by not being able to see him, and some days he was fine.

A few days passed, and before going to bed, Theresa was sitting at the computer in the computer room. While on the computer, she came across a video someone had posted on YouTube. It was a video of the rapture taking place. With her headphones over her ears, she watched and listened to the video. It showed people sitting in a church as the preacher was in the pulpit speaking, and right in the middle of his message, the people started to vanish one by one.

Everyone vanished except one man, who was left behind. The man stood and started looking around, wondering what was going on.

While watching the video, Theresa said, "Oh my God; this is something."

Although Theresa had heard things of the rapture, she was amazed to see that someone had made a video demonstrating it. Tarell heard Theresa as he was sitting on the computer room floor playing a game on his cell phone.

"What? Let me see!" he said, getting up off the floor.

"Hold up a minute," Theresa said.

"Come on, Theresa. Can I see?"

"Okay," she said while handing Tarell the headphones.

Tarell put the headphones over his ears as Theresa started the video over. As Tarell watched the video, a look of fear came over his face.

"Theresa," he said, "where did those people go?" Theresa could tell he was frightened. "Where did they go? And why was that one guy still standing there?" he asked.

"It's a demonstration of the rapture. The people went to Heaven and the guy standing there was left behind."

Confused and still very frightened, he asked, "What happened to the guy that was left behind? Theresa, what happened to him?"

"Calm down, Tarell. I shouldn't have let you watched that video."

"Theresa, please tell me what happened to that man; I need to know. Please!"

"He didn't make it in. He didn't go to Heaven."

"Theresa, please; I need you to contact the person that put that video up there and ask them what happened to that man."

"Tarell, you're getting yourself all worked up. Please calm down. Tarell, listen to me. The man was left behind because he wasn't one of God's people; he never gave his life to God. You grew up in church, so you know what it means when people say they got saved. He waited too late."

Theresa was shaken up after seeing what was happening with Tarell. She knew he had a disability, but she had no idea to what extent. She felt bad, and she kept telling herself she should have known.

"Theresa, please; I have to get saved," pleaded Tarell.

Before Theresa could say anything, he continued, "Please help me!!"

"Okay," said Theresa.

By this time, Tarell was down on his knees. Theresa spoke to him, saying, "Do you believe that Jesus Christ is the Son of God and that he died on the cross for your sins?"

"Yes, I believe it."

"Okay, now repeat after me... Lord I do believe..."

"Lord I do believe..."

"...That you sent your son Jesus into this world..."

"...That you sent your son Jesus into this world..."

"...To pay the price for my sins..."

"...To pay the price for my sins..."

"...So that I wouldn't have to."

"...So that I wouldn't have to."

Theresa continued, "I believe within my heart..."

"I believe within my heart," Tarell repeated.

"...That he was crucified and is alive today."

"...That he was crucified and is alive today."

She continued, "Tonight, I ask that you come into my heart as I receive you."

Tarell repeated.

Theresa, in closing, said, "In Jesus name, Amen," and Tarell repeated her.

"Okay, you are now saved," said Theresa, "and if the rapture were to take place while you and I are still on this earth, we won't be left behind."

"Okay," said Tarell.

After about a minute or so, Tarell said, "I'm not going to sleep tonight. I'm scared."

"Tarell, you don't have to be scared."

"But I am. Even after getting saved, I'm still scared."

"There's nothing to be scared about. God will always protect you."

"Can I sleep in the living room on the couch tonight?"

"You wanna sleep on that uncomfortable couch instead of in your bed?" Theresa asked.

"Yeah... please?" Tarell pleaded.

"Sure you can, if that's what you want."

"And can I keep the living room light on?"

"Yeah," she said, seeing the fear in his eyes.

Theresa thought to herself, *how could I have done something so stupid, showing him that video?*

That night, Tarell called Ms. Thomas.

"Mom, it's me, Jermaine."

"Hi, Jermaine; what are you still doing up? Is everything okay?"

"Mom, I saw a video on the computer and it was a lot of people in a church and the pastor was talking and then the people started disappearing, and only one man was still in the church. Theresa said it was the rapture and that God came to get his people and the man couldn't go because he went to Hell."

"Jermaine, calm down. You have to calm down."

"Ma, have you ever heard of this?"

"Yes, but don't worry yourself with that. Okay?"

"Okay."

"Try and get you some sleep, and let me speak to Theresa."

Tarell handed Theresa the phone.

"Hello," said Theresa.

"Hi, Theresa... Listen, Jermaine can't take seeing stuff like that. Even when it comes down to watching scary movies, he has nightmares and can't go to sleep. He went to the hospital one time when he was a child after watching something that scared him. You're going to have to watch him, and if you see that you need to call the ambulance to take him to the psychiatric hospital then you do it. In the time that he has been at your house, I don't know if you've noticed that he has some mental problems."

"Yes, I am aware of that. I just didn't know it was to that extent."

"Make sure you watch him because he's suicidal."

"I will."

That night, Tarell stayed up for hours, sitting on the couch with the light on. Theresa sat in a nearby chair reading the Bible to him, just as he had requested. She read until her eyes started giving out on her. Every time she would doze off, Tarell woke her up.

"Theresa, wake up."

"Oh, sorry... you're not tired?"

"No, just keep reading to me."

After a while, Tarell finally fell asleep. Very tired, Theresa went in her room and went to sleep as well.

The next morning, Tarell was better and as days went by, he had forgotten about the video altogether. Well, he never mentioned it, anyway.

Chapter Thirty Seven

It had been weeks since Tarell heard anything from Tina, but one day, she decided to call in the middle of the night.

"Hi, Tarell. What are you doing?"

"Nothing, just laying down, watching TV."

"I miss you," said Tina. "I was thinking maybe you should come back home."

"But I don't wanna come back home," he said.

"Don't you miss me? Don't you miss your son?" Tina asked.

"Yeah, I miss him. Can I speak to him?"

"He's sleep, but you can come see him if you'd like."

"Can you bring him over here to see me tomorrow?"

"No, I'm not bringing him over there, but you're welcome to come over here and see him. Why you acting like you don't miss me? Don't you miss me?"

"I don't know; I guess a little bit."

"Oh, you don't love me anymore? You can't just fall out of love with me that fast."

Tarell didn't respond.

Tina continued, "Tarell, I need you to come over here and be with me tonight. I'll pick you up. I'm horny; I need you, and I need some sex."

"No! Don't come over here. I don't wanna have sex with you."

"Oh, you having sex with someone else?" asked Tina.

"No, I'm not having sex with anyone," said Tarell.

"Are you having sex with that minister lady?"

"No, she's not like other ladies. She's like a mother to me, and Eric is like my father."

"Who's Eric?" Tina inquired.

"Theresa's husband," he answered.

"Oh, you and him are close?"

"Yeah, he talks to me a lot, just like a father and son. I'm saved now, too."

"Oooh... are you? That's good! So that means you've been studying the Bible some, so you *should* know that a husband's duty is to make sure his wife's needs are met, and I just told you that I'm horny and I need some sex from my husband," she said.

"But I don't wanna have sex with you; we're not even together," Tarell responded.

"But we are still married, and even if we're not together you are still supposed to make sure I'm satisfied sexually. You said you're saved, right? Well you need to do what saved husbands do."

Tarell didn't know what to say. He didn't know if Tina was telling the truth, so he told Tina to hold on a minute and pressed the mute button on his phone. He knocked on Theresa's door and she answered after being awakened.

"Who is it?"

"It's me, Tarell. Theresa, I need to talk to you."

"Hold on Tarell."

Theresa got out of her bed and put her robe on before opening her bedroom door.

"Theresa, my wife is on the phone, and she said she's coming to pick me up, but I don't want to go with her."

"Okay, then you don't have to."

"I told her that, but she's still gonna come. She's on the phone and she said even though we're not together, I'm still supposed to have sex with her."

"What??" Theresa was appalled at the ridiculousness she was hearing.

"I told her I was saved now, and she said saved husbands are supposed to know that."

"Give me the phone," Theresa said, but then changed her mind. "No, as a matter of fact, I'm not even going to go there. I don't believe this; just tell her you're not going over there."

Tarell un-muted the phone and said, "Hello?"

"What took you so long?" Tina asked.

"I had to do something, but I'm finished talking to you and don't come over here because I'm not going anywhere with you."

He hung up the phone.

Within seconds, his phone started ringing.

Speaking to Theresa he said, "That's her again but I'm not gonna answer it." Tarell turned his ringer off.

"Good night, Theresa."

"Good night, Tarell; try and get some sleep."

The next day, Tina kept calling his phone, but he ignored her calls. After a while, she stopped calling.

Five days passed, and she began calling again. Tarell was at the kitchen table eating when he answered her call.

"Why you doing me like this?" Tina asked. "I'm your wife and you're refusing to have sex with me, Tarell. I thought you liked having sex with me... I know you're having sex with that woman."

"No I'm not! I'm not having sex with Theresa," Tarell responded.

Surprised by what Tarell had said, Theresa said, "What did you just say?"

I know this trifling tramp ain't accusing him of sleeping with me, she thought.

"Tarell let me see that phone!!"

Tarell handed Theresa the phone.

"Listen, I don't know what your problem is, but I just want you to know that I'm not you. It's sad to see people so messed up that they would do these things to him. He's like a child."

"He's not a child; he's 22 years old," said Tina.

Theresa did not want Tarell to hear what she really wanted to say, so she said, "I'm not going to go there, but you're a grown woman in your forties and you have manipulated and used him terribly. What you have done to him and are still doing to him is wrong. You sleeping with him was straight up rape, no matter how you slice it."

Theresa was upset, and being from the streets, some of that ole' ghetto gangster came out of her.

"Rape?" Tina responded. "How can I be raping my own husband?" She laughed.

Theresa continued, "It's something, how a person can go to prison for sleeping with someone underage, not knowing any better... but then you have people that know better, and they manipulate and sleep with a disabled person, and they don't get the same treatment. It's insane; it's crazy! Only excuse for that is if the person that's doing it is insane herself."

"Oh, you're calling me insane?" Tina laughed.

"A person in their right mind would do the right thing. That's all I'm saying," said Theresa.

Tina, like so many people in today's society, didn't know that rape is not only done by force, but by deception as well. Even with the other party being a willing participate, as Tarell was later in the marriage. In other words, a person can be manipulated or deceived by another person and willingly give themselves to that person not realizing or knowing they are being deceived, and an act of rape is committed. Although the law doesn't get into all of this, knowing the meaning of rape, God does. But when you have a disabled person being manipulated and deceived by a "sane" person, something really needs to be done, even by the law.

"If you married him for love, then you would be there for him," Theresa began. "You would help him, and you would teach him because he's never been taught a lot of things. I'm not trying to judge you because I myself didn't do a lot of things in life I should have done. But in realizing my mistakes, I'm only trying to tell you that you're not helping him; you're doing more damage to him than before he came to you. And it's not just you, but all the other women he has come across. This is what he knows of women. Tarell looked to you as a mother and you manipulated him and then married him. He doesn't know anything about being somebody's husband."

Tina stayed quiet the whole time Theresa spoke, and when she stopped, Tina simply said, "Yeah, okay, whatever," and hung up.

Tina's way of helping Tarell was by not calling him. Tarell never heard from her again. And by the same token, he never heard from his son, either. Tarell went around the house many days sad as he thought about his son, but he eventually learned how to cope with it. He could have gone to court to get visitation, but decided he didn't want to do that.

When his son's 3rd birthday came around, he tried to call Tina but her number had changed. That day, Tarell felt down because he couldn't tell his son "Happy Birthday!"

As he entered the kitchen where Theresa was cooking, she could see he had a lot on his mind.

"What's with the long face? I don't like seeing you like that. I know it's your son's birthday, and I know it's not easy."

Theresa knew the feeling, because although she

had made peace with her son Bryan being gone, every year on his birthday she had the same feelings.

She continued, "I know it's been a rough road, but God is good and you have to give Him thanks anyhow. Your son is in good hands. He's in God's hands. You have many things to be grateful for and one day you will realize that. In everything that you've been through, God has been there and he protected you. Even in the midst of everything that's still going on, he hasn't forgotten about you. He's going to one day take all your sorrows and turn them into a beautiful tomorrow. You just wait and see."

Tarell was looking at Theresa with a half smile on his face.

Theresa, smiling, said, "Cheer up...life is a wonderful thing and it's God who gave it to us."

Tarell's smile deepened.

"Okay, that's what I'm talking about. I have an idea. Tarell, each day, why don't you write down the things that are on your mind? Whatever it is you're thinking about that day, write it down, and when we pray at night, we'll bring it up to God, or you can bring it up to God when you pray alone."

"You think I should write down the things that I'm thinking about?" said Tarell.

"Yes, I do. I think it will help. It always helps me to write down the things that are on my mind. Sometimes I can't talk to people about them, so it's just easier for me to write them down. When I write them, it feels like I'm talking to God and expressing what I'm feeling inside to Him. Also, it helps me to remember all the things I need to bring up when I talk to Him in prayer."

"Okay, I'm going to my room to write them down," said Tarell.

"Who knows, Tarell? Maybe even one day your story will be a book," said Theresa.

"Do you think so?"

"Yes. Anything is possible through God. All it takes is written thoughts—yours and God's."

Tarell headed out of the kitchen, excited about writing out his thoughts. As he was leaving out the kitchen, Theresa said, "While you're writing, don't forget to think about all the good things God has done for you and don't forget to thank him."

"Okay, I will."

Unfortunately, he couldn't think of anything. He came back into the kitchen about 30 minutes later with a piece of paper in his hand.

"I wrote out what I was thinking. You wanna read it?"

"Sure, if you don't mind."

"No, I don't mind."

He handed the paper to Theresa, and she started to read it. He had about fifteen lines written on the paper. As Theresa read it, Tarell explained, "It's a song."

Over the top heading it read, "Dream."

"Oh, you wrote a song!"

"Yeah, you like it?"

"Yeah, but you have to sing it so I can hear how it goes."

Tarell sang what he had written.

"Yeah, I like it. I like it a lot. Maybe I can speak to my brother and let him hear you sing, and maybe he can bring you into the studio. He's into music."

"Going into the studio sounds good, but I don't trust people because they just be wanting you to be in the studio singing all day, and they don't give you nothing," said Tarell.

"Huh?" Theresa responded.

"I went into a studio before and sung a lot of songs for these guys, and they said they were gonna give me some money but they didn't. I asked them for money to eat with because I was hungry and they still didn't give it to me," explained Tarell.

"Oh, I understand. But just so you know, I wouldn't let nobody take advantage of you if you would to go into a studio."

"I know. If I would to go into a studio and sing for someone, I would want you to be my manager."

"Okay, sounds good to me," she said in agreement.

Tarell smiled. "I know they ain't gonna be able to get over on you."

"You got that right," said Theresa as she laughed.

In being distracted with all that they were talking about, Tarell's mind wandered from the things that had him feeling down earlier. He was in good spirits for the rest of that day.

That evening before dinner, Tarell came into the kitchen to make himself a sandwich. He opened the refrigerator to get the jelly out, and opened the loaf of bread that was on the table. He took two slices from it.

Theresa saw that he only had the jelly spread on the bread with no peanut butter.

"I heard of people eating peanut butter and jelly but I haven't come across to many people that like jelly sandwiches."

Tarell laughed and said, "I like peanut butter."

"Oh, but you just decided to have a jelly sandwich today?" Theresa asked.

Tarell continued to smile because Theresa was being humorous when she spoke, not realizing that Tarell didn't know how to make a peanut butter and jelly sandwich.

"Get the peanut butter from the cabinet," said Theresa.

Tarell opened the cabinet and reached for the peanut butter.

"Okay," she said as she took two more slices of bread from the loaf, "watch how I do it."

Theresa began to spread the peanut butter on the bread. "Now you try it," she said to Tarell after she finished.

When Tarell tried, he broke the bread.

"Okay, Tarell, I see what you're doing wrong; you have to take your time. Don't be so rough with trying to put the peanut butter on the bread. If you do, it's going to break."

Tarell tried again, but again, the bread broke.

"Okay, maybe I just need to buy some smoother peanut butter," said Theresa.

"All the peanut butters are like that," said Tarell.

"Every time I put peanut butter on bread that happens."

"Okay, try it again; take your time and spread it slow."

"No, it's gonna break again, Theresa. You just do it for me."

"No, no, no, you do it. Don't you wanna learn how to do it yourself?"

"Yeah, but I just know the bread is gonna break again."

"Ok, and if that should happen, we'll just try it again until you get it," said Theresa.

After going through half of the loaf, Tarell finally got it, and soon afterwards, he mastered it.

As Theresa helped him, she thought about her son Bryan, who also had a hard time making sandwiches, and who she didn't teach. She thought about how she would make it for him, and when he would try to make it himself, the other kids would laugh at how it looked.

After Tarell ate his sandwich, he called Ms. Thomas to see how she was doing. It had been a while since he last spoke with her. As Ms. Thomas answered, Tarell said, "Hi, Ma."

Once she recognized his voice, Ms. Thomas said, "Hi Jermaine."

"I just called to see how you were doing; I haven't spoken to you in a while."

"Yeah, I know. I've just been going through a lot, but I'm hanging in there."

"How is everybody else doing?" Tarell asked.

"Everybody's doing okay, I guess."

"Ma, guess what?"

"What?"

"My wife still has my food stamp card; she never gave it to me. That day when she was on the phone when I first came to Theresa's house, she said she used the money to buy food for her house."

Ms. Thomas didn't know that Tarell had her on speaker. Theresa was standing at the kitchen sink doing dishes and listening to the conversation.

"That's some bullshit!" she exclaimed. "What does she mean she used them to put food in her house? You weren't there at her house. She ain't doing nothing but telling a damn lie."

Tarell muted the phone, looked at Theresa, and started laughing. "I told you she curses," he said, then unmuted the phone.

Ms. Thomas continued, "She probably gets her own food stamps and she probably just sold yours."

"Yeah, but it's okay because I sent for a new card. Well Ma, I'm gonna let you go. I'll talk to you another time."

"Okay," said Ms. Thomas, "I love you."

"I love you too, Mom."

After hanging up the phone, Tarell said, "Told you that she curses; you didn't believe me."

"It's not that I didn't believe you, Tarell, I was just surprised to hear that. I was surprised even in hearing her cursing just now, but to God be the glory."

"What does that mean?" Tarell asked.

"It means that whatever takes place with a person,

whether it is something wrong or right, God is still gonna get what He needs to get out of the person. It's something like when I said that we needed to try to see the good things that people do instead of all the bad things. Remember when I told you that?"

"Yeah."

"Okay, well God sees the good things in a person, and he wants other people to see them, too. And when other people see them, the things that that person is doing wrong won't matter much. Well, they won't matter to us, anyway, because what we see is the good. If people see the good in a person, they won't treat the person badly just because they're doing something wrong. But I don't mean you," Theresa smiled, "because I know you treat everybody good, and it makes God happy."

She continued, "Then, Tarell, what sometimes ends up happening is that person that was doing the wrong things will stop doing them because of all the love that people showed them by being nice to them. In other words, no matter what a person does wrong, we still love them, and God still loves them, and He's not going to give up on them."

"Yeah, I understand. After everything that Ms. Thomas does wrong, I still love her. I really do, and I don't know why, but I just do," said Tarell.

Theresa smiled.

Chapter Thirty Eight

Every weekend, the young adult children in the neighborhood would come over to Theresa's house to eat. These were young people that Theresa's children had grown up with. Besides Theresa's two teenagers, Darren and Kenneth, who lived in the house, and Bryan, Theresa had two other children, Desiree, who was twenty-one and Craig who was twenty-two. Both had their own apartments but would still come over. Then there was Faze, the sixteen-year-old who seemed to be going through so many different phases in his young life. Faze lived around the corner from Theresa but would come over Theresa's house most of the time. He was like Theresa's own child, and people often thought he was. He even had his own room at her house.

Faze came from a home where his mother was never really around. They all loved Theresa's food and looked forward to it on the weekends. Some of the children came from homes where the parents didn't cook, and some came from homes where there was no food to cook.

However, there were reasons behind this. Some came from homes with single mothers who worked a lot and didn't have time to cook. Then, there were some who came from homes where the mothers were just too busy hanging out, and had no money for food after spending it on the nightlife. There were also mothers that were on drugs, and some were even disabled. But whatever the case, these young people knew they could always come to eat at Theresa's house. All the parents of these children were single mothers. Theresa knew she wasn't only helping these children, but she felt that she was filling in for the mothers by helping them, whether they realized it or not.

Tarell got to meet the young people whose ages ranged from sixteen to around nineteen, aside from Desiree and Craig, who were a little older than the others. Tarell enjoyed being around them.

Faze, along with a couple of the other teenagers, called Theresa "Mom." His real name was Jamel, but he preferred the nickname that his friends had given him.

Since Tarell heard some of the young people calling Theresa "Mom," he said, "Theresa, I wanna ask you something."

"Ok, what is it?" Theresa asked.

"No, it may be kind of silly."

"I'm sure it's not. What is it?"

"I was thinking to ask you if I could call you Mom."

Theresa half laughed and said, "Is that all? You were scared to ask me that?"

"Yeah, because I didn't know what you were gonna say; it's just that you are like a mother and you're a good mother. Your kids are lucky. I thought Faze was your real son. He always calls you Mom, and he be over here every day."

"Yes... he's just like one of my own children."

"At first, Theresa, I thought Nicole was your real daughter, but then she told me she wasn't."

"Yes a lot of them call me Mom, and that's because they look at me to be old and they're young." Theresa laughed.

"I like when they come over. We have a lot of fun. That's when I have the most fun because they're funny. They be cracking on each other, making me laugh," he said.

Jokingly, Theresa said, "Oh, so my house is boring when they're not here?"

"No, I didn't mean it like that."

Theresa laughed and said, "I'm just joking with you, but to answer your question, I don't mind you calling me Mom. My oldest son is twenty-eight, so it's okay. But anybody that's older than my son, I would have to think about that one."

"Thanks, Mom!" Tarell was so happy to hear Theresa's answer and he kept a big smile on his face. From that day forth, he referred to Theresa as "Mom," and not just in private; he called her "Mom" everywhere they went.

Chapter Thirty Nine

Tarell stayed at Theresa's house three years. His son was now five years old. Tarell had learned all the things needed in life for him to be successful and to take care of himself. He learned so much that he was no longer identified as being EMR or even disabled. He was very involved in the church and had even taken one of the weeknight classes at the church that was offered. The class he attended was a fatherhood class, held for an hour every Tuesday night. In this class, men would come together and learn about being a good father.

While at Theresa's house, he enrolled in school for Computer Science and received an Associate's Degree. He still attended school part-time as he pursued his career.

Tarell ended up getting a job making $50,000 a year. The company wanted him badly because they saw how knowledgeable he was when it came to computers. Normally, they started their employees off with $40,000 a year, but Tarell was the exception.

He later moved out of Theresa's house and into his

own place. He bought himself a nice two-bedroom condominium in North Haven, CT, and was finally able to put the past behind him and move on with his life. He was finally living the life he had always desired, and soon, his life superseded what he could have even imagined existed. He had a life of peace, joy, forgiveness and love.

Now that he had gotten on his feet and had his life in order, he thought about contacting a lawyer to get some kind of visitation rights with his son. However, after three months of being in his condo, he got a call from child welfare.

"Hello?"

"Hi, can I speak with Jermaine Thomas?"

"This is Jermaine Thomas."

"My name is Susan Santana and I'm calling from child welfare. I was wondering if I can stop by this afternoon so we can talk."

"Sure. Is everything all right? Does this have anything to do with my son?"

"Yes it does, but he's fine. I'll explain when I come see you. Are you going to be available around 3pm?"

"Yes, I can be. I'm at work, but I can leave and meet with you."

"Oh, you're at work. No, that won't be necessary. What time do you get off?"

"4:30."

"Okay, then we can meet at 5:30 if that's okay."

"Yes, that will be fine," said Tarell.

"I'll come to your house," said Ms. Santana.

Before hanging up, he gave Ms. Santana his address. On his way home, he called Theresa.

"Mom," he said.

"Yes?" Theresa responded.

"I just got a call from a woman from child welfare"

Before Tarell could say anything else, Theresa asked, "About what?"

"She didn't say. I have an appointment with her in about thirty minutes. She said it has to do with my son, but said he's OK." He paused for a second, and then continued. "Anyway, Mom, let me go; I'm pulling up in my driveway now. I'll call you after the meeting."

"Ok," said Theresa.

About twenty minutes after Tarell arrived at his condo, Ms. Santana arrived and rang the doorbell.

"Just a minute," Tarell said as he made his way to the door.

"Hi, I'm Ms. Santana."

"Hi, come in and have a seat," he said as he led her into the living room.

"Thank you," she said as she sat down. "This is a nice place you have!"

"Thank you," Tarell said.

"Okay, let me tell you the reason I'm here. Your son is in the custody of child welfare. I don't know how long it's been since you've spoken to your wife.... or is she your ex-wife?"

"Tina, she's my wife; we've been separated about 3 years, but I haven't seen or spoken to her in that time."

"Oh, I see," said Ms. Santana. After a long pause, she said, "Your wife passed away a couple of days ago."

"Passed away?"

Tarell was in complete shock. He had known she was infected with the virus, but when he heard she passed away it took him back. Tarell went to the doctor to get checked shortly after he arrived at Theresa's house, and had been going every six months after that. All the test results came back negative.

"I'm sorry about your wife, Mr. Thomas."

Tarell gave a little smile then said, "Thank you."

"She died from AIDS," Ms. Santana continued.

"How's my son doing?"

"He's doing okay."

"He's been with his mother since he was born. This has to be hard for him," said Tarell.

"Well, for the most part, he's doing okay, but he's been asking for her. Before she died, and while in the hospital, she gave one of the social workers your phone number. So you haven't seen your son in 3 years either?"

"No, I haven't."

"Well, you're his next of kin, and besides that, I believe your wife wanted him to be with you. I had a brief conversation with the social worker that visited your wife, and she shared with me that in the last conversation they had, your wife's biggest concern was that you and your son be reunited. If you're able to care for your son then we will bring him to you. His sister Debbie has been coming to the agency to check on him. She informed us that if you're not able to care for him, then she would be willing to take custody of him. She was given custody of her sister, Shakira."

"Oh no, that won't be necessary. I'm able to take care of my son. I have two bedrooms and I make more than enough money to support him," Tarell stated.

"You said you have two bedrooms here?"

"Yes."

"Can I take a look?"

"Sure," Tarell said as he got up to lead her to the fully furnished bedroom that he had decorated himself 3 months ago, imagining that Tina would one day allow his son to come and visit.

"Okay, Mr. Thomas. I'll be dropping your son off to you tomorrow. Is that okay?"

"Yes, that's more than okay. I can't wait to see him."

Ms. Santana smiled and left.

Shortly after Ms. Santana left, he got on the phone to call Theresa to tell her about what just happened.

"Mom, the social worker just left. She said my wife died."

"Oh my God!" said Theresa.

"Yeah, the social worker said she died from AIDS two days ago, and my son is in the state's custody. She asked me if I would be willing to take him and raise him. I told her yes, so she's going to drop him off tomorrow after I get out of work!"

"Tarell, you're going to be a great father."

"Yeah, I can't wait to see him. He probably doesn't remember me."

"I'm sure he does. Even being that young, most times they remember their parents. You know I'm here if you need me."

"I know... Thanks. I should call out from work tomorrow, but then again, I'd better wait. I have to find out what day the funeral is going to be because I'm going to have to take that day off."

"That poor girl," said Theresa, "It's so sad to hear that. God have mercy."

"Yes, it is sad. It's kind of hard to believe. When I see the social worker tomorrow, I'll get the funeral information, or I'll ask her for Debbie's number. That's Tina's daughter. Well, Mom, I'll talk to you tomorrow."

"Okay. Are you going to be alright, Tarell?"

"Yes Mom; I'll be fine."

"Goodnight, Tarell. I love you."

"Goodnight. I love you too."

The next evening, after Tarell got home from work, the social worker dropped little Tarell off to his father's home.

"Hi Tarell," said Tarell, Sr. "Do you remember me?"

Tarell, Jr. looked up at him and bashfully put his head down.

"Have a seat Ms. Santana," said Tarell, Sr.

"Oh, I'm not going to stay long. I only came to drop your son off and to go over a few other things with you."

"Oh okay."

"I just want to let you know that if you need to contact us, we're here to assist you."

"Thank you; I appreciate that," said Tarell, humbled.

"Come here, little Tarell," he said.

Tarell Jr. walked over to him and Tarell picked him up.

"Okay, I'm going to leave now," said Ms. Santana. "Good luck with your son."

"Thank you, and thanks for everything."

"You're very welcome, Mr. Thomas."

Ms. Santana headed towards the front door to leave, but before she exited, Tarell said, "Oh, Ms. Santana; would you happen to have any information concerning the funeral?"

"Yes I do, actually. I spoke with Tina's daughter, Debbie, and she told me the funeral is going to be this coming Monday. Hold on a minute; let me get the information she gave me."

Ms. Santana stuck her hand in her pocketbook to find the piece of paper she had written the information on. After finding it, she handed it to Tarell.

"Thank you," said Tarell as he took the piece of paper.

"You're welcome," she said, and then left.

Tarell was so happy to see his son.

"How are you, Tarell?" he asked. "You just don't know how much I miss you, man. You're going to be staying here with me. Is that okay with you, little man?"

Tarell, Jr. didn't say anything.

"Oh don't tell me you're shy. You didn't used to be shy. I'm your father... but you already knew that... right?"

Still, Tarell, Jr. gave no response.

"Do you wanna watch TV for a little while?" Tarell asked as he turned the living room television on. "You hungry or did you already eat something?"

Tarell Jr. remained silent.

"Oh, you don't want to talk. Okay, when you're ready, let me know. In the meantime, I'm going to put some cartoons on."

Tarell turned the channel to cartoons. The both of them sat watching Scooby Doo. After a while, little Tarell started laughing. Tarell, Sr. looked over at him and was glad to see his son smile.

When they were finished watching the cartoons Tarell made the both of them something to eat. He had learned how to cook many different dishes while living at Theresa's house, but had decided that he would make something quick, so he made cheeseburgers and French fries. When they were finished eating, Tarell gave his son a bath and then took his night clothes out of the packed bag that the social worker had dropped off with him.

After Tarell put the night clothes on Tarell, Jr., Tarell escorted him to his room. The room was pretty large and nicely decorated with an Elmo sheet set and comforter. The walls were painted white and had pictures of Elmo drawn directly on them by an artist. There was a complete full-sized bedroom set in the room and a white wooden chair in a corner of the room.

After putting his son to bed and giving him a kiss, Tarell turned the light off, but there was still a little light coming into the room from the nightlight that was plugged into the wall. Tarell was so overwhelmed with joy that he sat in the white wooden chair in his son's room and just watched him from a distance. While sitting in the chair, Tarell was in deep thought. He thought about how he always hoped to be able to see his son and spend time with him, but he never thought in a million years that things would happen the way they did; he never imagined that Tina would die and he would be left to raise his son. When Tarell Jr. was sound asleep, Tarell left the room after he gave him another kiss on his forehead. Tired, Tarell got in the shower and went to bed.

That next day, Tarell called out from work. It was Friday and Fridays on the job weren't too busy. They went to a park, which Tarell, Jr. really seemed to enjoy. It didn't take long before he came out of his shell.

Tarell, Jr. enjoyed spending time with his father but often asked about his mother. Tarell didn't take him by Theresa's house that weekend, knowing how busy it got during weekends at her house. He didn't want to overwhelm him with all the excitement and the multitude of people...not just yet, anyway. He called Theresa to tell her he'd be by to introduce her to Tarell, Jr. after the funeral on Monday.

On Monday, Tarell accompanied his son to the funeral. He could have gone by himself and asked Theresa to watch Tarell, Jr. since she had decided not to attend, but he felt it was best that he be there. However, he decided not to let Tarell, Jr. Look into the casket.

While sitting there in the church, Tarell saw a lot of Tina's family members, the same ones who attended the BBQ's and the Thanksgiving dinners that were held at Tina's mother's house. People were going up to the casket to view the body. Tarell made his way up to the front of the church to view Tina's body. Many tears were shed as people made their way to the front.

"Excuse me. Can you keep an eye on my son?" Tarell asked the lady next to him.

"Sure I can," said the woman.

As Tarell stood over the casket looking at his wife, he saw that Tina didn't look anything like herself; she was no more than 100 pounds. As he stood over her, negative thoughts went through his mind, but he fought to think positive thoughts. Tarell became good at that through the years, not dwelling on the bad and only seeing the good.

He thought about how through it all, he really did care about Tina. Then he thought about how he would put a rose on her pillow when she was upset, hoping it would cheer her up. While looking over in the casket, he said, "I love you, and God loves you."

As he made his way back to his seat, he thought to himself,

Today, I can truly say I love her now that I know what love is. I have God's love in me, and I was able to love not even understanding what love really was.

It's something how a person can still show love and not even understand it, but when you understand it, it's even far greater.

Tarell's heart was filled with nothing but love.

When the funeral was over and the people were leaving, they greeted one another. Tarell spoke with some of Tina's family members. He spoke with Tina's mother and gave her his number just in case she wanted to call or see her grandson.

When he and Debbie saw one another, they greeted each other with a hug.

"Hi Tarell," she said as she gave a little smile.

"Hey Debbie," he said as he smiled back.

"How have you been?" Debbie asked.

"I've been good, and yourself?"

"I've been okay; it's good seeing you."

"Same here."

Everything about Tarell was different and Debbie noticed it right away. She noticed a difference in the way he carried himself and the clothes he wore. Tarell's black two-piece Christian Dior suit with his light burgundy shirt and matching tie, black snakeskin shoes and dark Versace shades made it clear that he was a man of distinction. There was no question that Tarell was as handsome as he had always been. Debbie observed how well Tarell wore the fine clothes he had on, and not to mention, the way he spoke.

Tarell noticed that Debbie eyes were red from crying, so he said, "I'm sorry about what happened with your mother."

"Yeah, it's sad. I didn't even know she was sick

until eight months ago; that's when everything started going downhill with her. I spent a lot of time with her in those months. She didn't want you to see her like that, and that's why she didn't contact you."

"I wish she had, but it's OK. She had her reasons," Tarell said.

"Hi baby," Debbie said to Tarell, Jr.,

"I hear you're going to be living with your dad. Don't you forget about your big sister, OK?"

"OK," said Tarell Jr.

"I love you," she continued as she kissed him.

"I love you too," he said.

"Debbie, you can see him whenever you'd like."

Debbie smiled and said, "Thank you, but I think for now, you need this time with just you and him. Take care, Tarell and take care of my little brother."

"I will; he's in good hands," Tarell said as he gave a friendly smile. "And you take care of yourself, too."

Debbie watched Tarell and Tarell, Jr. as they walked to the church parking lot and got into a brand new 2007 760 BMW. After Tarell strapped Tarell, Jr's seatbelt, they drove away.

While he drove, Tarell thought about what Theresa had said that day over two years ago in the kitchen. He remembered when she told him to think about all the good things that God had done for him and write them down and thank Him. He realized that he never thought about it, nor did he write them down, or even thank God, for that matter. He thought about Theresa's words when she told him God was always with him, and that God will one day turn his sorrows into a beautiful tomorrow. After he arrived home, he saw that Tarell, Jr. had fallen asleep. He unstrapped the seat belt and carried him inside. He took his shoes off and laid him down on his bed.

Tarell went into the kitchen, got a pen and a piece of paper out of one of the kitchen drawers and then sat down at the table. He began to write out his list of all the things he was thankful for.

God, I am thankful for being alive.

I'm thankful, God, that you have allowed me to see and understand.

Thank you for being with me and letting me know that you've always been with me.

Thank you for the peace you've given me in these latter years.

Thanks for my biological parents who gave me natural life.

I am thankful for my adoptive mother, who took me in even through her own trials, and took me to church every Sunday, as I was introduced to you.

I'm so thankful to you, Lord, that you placed Theresa in my life; she's a woman with a big heart that taught me and showed me nothing but love and wanted nothing from me in return. Instead, she wanted something for me—peace and happiness.

I'm thankful, God, for my child and for Tina, the mother of my child. May she rest in peace.

I'm so thankful that my son will never have to

*experience the things I have, and with all that is in
me through you, he will have.*

*Lord, thank you for seeing all my sorrows and
turning them into a beautiful tomorrow. Sincerely, I
am thankful and grateful.*

Later that evening, Tarell went to Theresa's
house to introduce Tarell, Jr. to her and to thank
her for everything. He had thanked her many times
before, but just wanted to thank her again. While at
Theresa's house, she offered him something to eat.

"No, I'm alright," said Tarell. "I only stopped by
for a few minutes."

"Okay, well while you're here, let me give this
precious baby some cookies and milk."

Theresa reached for the cookies on the second
shelf in the cabinet, and then took the milk out the
refrigerator.

"Come here, Sweetie; you want some cookies and
milk? Come sit right here at the table."

Theresa gave him three cookies and a cup of
milk. Tarell, Jr. sat there happily as he enjoyed the
cookies.

"So how are you, Tarell?" Theresa asked Tarell,
Sr.

"I'm doing alright. No, let me take that back. I'm a
little nervous; all this is new to me. But, other than
that, I'm doing well and I'm feeling good."

"You'll be fine," said Theresa. "You'll be just
fine."

"Thank you," Tarell said with gratitude.

"Thank you for everything," he continued.

Reaching in his pocket, he pulled out the piece of

paper that he had written on earlier that day. As he handed it to Theresa, he said, "This is the "Thank You" list for the things God has done for me."

Reminded of that day in the kitchen over two years ago, Theresa smiled as she took the paper into her hands and began to read what he had written. With tears in her eyes, she continued to read. When she was finished, she was speechless. She looked at him in amazement.

Tarell smiled and signaled his son to come to him.

Tarell, Jr. went to his father. Tarell then hugged Theresa and said, "I'll talk to you later. I love you."

"I love you too, Tarell," Theresa said with tears in her eyes.

This was the first time Tarell had witnessed an emotional side of Theresa. She was a strong woman and he had never seen tears in her eyes. However, these days, there was no confusion in how he saw things. He knew her tears were tears of joy.

She then kissed Tarell, Jr. and watched as they walked outside. Tarell and his son got in the car and headed home. When they arrived, Tarell got out of the car, removed his son's seatbelt and held his hand as they walked towards the condominium complex.

THE END!!!

This book was not written to degrade or disrespect anyone. It's no secret that today's society is infected with the curse of abuse. Abuse is abuse, no matter how you slice it or where it's coming from. It's happening in today's society; where a woman can come across a "good" man and doesn't recognize him as being a "good" man because she's so blinded and used to being with messed up, low-life men and she ends up abusing him and eventually losing him. Same goes for a man; he can come across a "good" woman and because he's so used to being with messed up, low-life women, he doesn't recognize her worth and he abuses her and eventually ends up losing her. I pray that God removes the blindness that consumes each and every person that cannot see the truth when it's presented before them. God bless!

"Words in Tarell's thoughts; written through the author..."

Prayer of Thanks

Lord, humbly I come to you, wanting to give you thanks. I spoke with you the other day, and today I have no complaints. My heart is filled with peace and joy in the presence of your mist; you told me to trust in you and everyday will be like this. Thank you Lord for your goodness, grace and tolerance. "Keep the faith," You said, as it will bring forth my deliverance. And in doing my part, I promised you, Lord, to keep seeking after your righteousness. My heart is so overwhelmed, enjoying you in happiness. Your words have always been said to me that you would work it out, and not to forget to practice patience and let your will play out.

A. Adams Jones

"Words in Tarell's thoughts; written through the author..."

<u>Forgiveness</u>

*Even when it comes down to forgiveness, God is willing to help us with this. Listen carefully, my friend, because you wouldn't want to miss this. Forgiveness is required no matter what a person has said or done. Ask God; He'll tell you all about it from what was done to his only begotten son. But just too briefly enlighten you on some of what took place, although it's hard to even talk about, we must remember that day; how he was crucified and left to die as his friends ran away. See, Jesus himself, went through all this, so know that he can relate. The physical abuse and being falsely accused is something people go through even today, but we must be like Christ, and in spite of it all, out of love, "**forgive**" anyway.*

A. Adams Jones

"Words in Tarell's thoughts; written through the author..."

<u>Love is the Message</u>

Many put on a show and act like they care;
They will even take you in and act like they want
you there.
But after awhile, their true colors come out and
then you see what they are really about.
So sad to see many people amongst me,
Abusing one another, something done so freely.
God gives us free will,
But we abuse it still, as we make our decisions
based on how we feel.
This is not God. Come on people; let's get real.
It's about love. You know the drill;
There's no other way, it's a package deal.
So soften your hearts and stop acting hard,
As many today are so far away from God.
Love is the message that I continue to speak,
I just want to see everyone experience God's
peace.

A. Adams Jones

Authors Notes on Mental Health

As <u>Blind Innocence</u> *gave some information on EMR, which is a mild level of mental retardation, there are also three more categories of mental retardation: moderate, severe, and profound.*

Although there are only four categories in total, there are many different degrees.

A person diagnosed with EMR, (which stands for educable mentally retarded) has an IQ in range of 50-70. As these individuals have impairment, they are capable of learning. Unlike a typical child, they may take longer to learn language, develop social skills, and take care of their personal needs, such as dressing themselves or even eating. Learning will take them longer, require more repetition, and skills may need to be adapted to their learning.

Nevertheless, virtually every child with EMR is capable of learning, developing, living independently and becoming a participating member of the community. They can learn to cook, travel and even maintain gainful employment.

A person with EMR can be educated up to a sixth grade level, which in age would be up to a 12 year old. A mild mental condition such as EMR is not detected until the child reaches school age, which is around 6 years old. Even when poor academic performance is recognized, it may take expert assessment to distinguish a mild mental condition such as EMR.

EMR is a learning disability and may in some

cases have some emotional/behavioral disorders as well.

Studies show that without some source of community/family support and direction, a person with EMR is at serious risk for failure in society, especially within the urban society, and are frequently seen as society's "misfits" who, if not simply ridiculed, are apt to be taken advantage of in serious ways because of their relative lack of interpersonal coping skills. So, family support and professional guidance can also simultaneously serve both therapeutic and prevention goals.

Teaching a person with EMR can be challenging, but ultimately, quite rewarding. They are able to learn so much, and in some cases, like Tarell's, are no longer identified as being EMR or even disabled.

As the author of <u>Blind Innocence</u> and having friends as well as close family members that were diagnosed with EMR, it led me to write this story and also conduct countless hours of research pertaining to EMR. For more information regarding EMR and the other categories of mental retardation, you can go to the "Mental Retardation Encyclopedia of Childhood and Adolescence."

Part Two coming soon

About the Author

Alfreda Adams Jones was born in Brooklyn NY, but was raised in Queens, the majority of her adolescent life. Returning to Brooklyn at the age of 17, she resided there until she reached age twenty-two. She then relocated to Connecticut. Alfreda grew up in a home with a mother who was a church goer and minister, and a father who came from a strong Christian background. Although she attended church throughout her childhood life, at the age of 20, while still living in Brooklyn and being exposed to the streets, she eventually got drawn into that life style and soon afterwards landed in a Connecticut state prison at the age of 22.

Being sentence to 5 to 10 years, she was released after 2 years. Still being in her darkness, and living the street life after her release, she continued to experience so many different trials in her life. At the age of 35, her life took a turn into another direction. Taking heed to her cousin's Myra's words while on her deathbed, that it was time to change her life, A.

Adams Jones eyes became opened. From that day forth she saw another outlook on life. She began to change her ways and make better decisions in her life. Her eyes were not only opened as to her own life, but to the lives of others. She later became an ordained minister and focused her life on helping others. She helps in assisting the homeless, single parents and is an advocate for inmates in three different states. She spends a lot of her time with the youth in her neighborhood encouraging them, and takes up time with the mentally challenged that are capable of learning and teaches them how to live independently, as well as the physically disabled that can't afford the health care that's needed to assist them; taking them into her home and caring for them. Amongst many other things that she is involved in; as to uplifting people that are faced with everyday struggles in life, she has dedicated her life to doing what God has called her upon.

Today, she knows without any doubts that she was placed on this earth for a purpose and is humbled to her calling.

All that she speaks about in what God has equipped her to do does not come from self-boasting, but simply that God may be glorified through her life.

Printed in the United States
By Bookmasters